THE INTRUDERS

BRETT MCKAY

The Intruders

Red Adept Publishing, LLC

104 Bugenfield Court

Garner, NC 27529

https://RedAdeptPublishing.com/

---

1.   http://StreetlightGraphics.com

Foreword

Thank you for purchasing *The Intruders*. I had a lot of fun writing this novel. I amped up the suspense, action, and horror in this story that I hope you won't be able to put down.

The Intruders first appeared on Amazon's new Vella platform in May of 2021 as a serialized novel, releasing one episode per week. The program was something new and exciting, and I had just finished writing the book, which was originally titled *The Strangers*, and because of its fast-pasted action and suspense, I felt it was a perfect fit for the new platform.

My favorite part about Vella was having the ability to add an author's note at the end of each episode. I could foreshadow coming events or write some fun facts about my journey. I did a little of both. When you let a writer talk about what he loves to do, it's hard to shut them up, so I took full advantage.

Coming up with those notes stirred memories that go back as far as eighteen years, when the concept of this story first emerged. It also took me to the home I lived in at the time. My kids were just rug rats then. I traveled a lot for work until I chose to give up a high-paying career and get a job closer to home, a choice I do not regret. But the only job I could find was selling cars, just like my main character, Dex. Those were rough days. With the up-and-down commissions, we found ourselves eating steak one month and beans the next. Mostly beans.

By publishing *The Intruders* as an ebook, I get the best of both worlds. I've also included all my author's notes. This makes it a unique, special edition that stands out from the rest of my novels. I enjoyed this experience, and I hope to do more Vella stories in the future.

I won't bore you any further. Get to reading. This story is explosive.

Chapter 1: The Stranger

On the last day that he would experience a life anything close to normal, Dex Sanders closed the car lot at a place he'd never return to. He wouldn't miss it. Not his job, anyway. Car sales was not his thing, and this job had been temporary at best. He was in between jobs, as he liked to say, not knowing where he'd end up, but he was in desperate need of a career change.

Dex strode through the car lot filled with Lincoln and Mercury vehicles, checking each door handle. Night had fallen, and Dex as well as his co-worker John, both eager to bust out of there, were speeding through their duties of securing the lot.

A cool breeze blew through the summer air. It was a fitting end to a hot afternoon. Dex finished his burn day for the week. "Burn day" was what people in the business called a shift that started at the opening and finished at the closing. He was mentally exhausted after suffering the most frustrating day of his sales career thus far. Not one customer had come, making him ready to crawl out of his skin and run down the street screaming. He'd felt trapped, like being stuck on the tarmac for hours, unable to deplane an aircraft.

Each door handle clicked as he checked it, and he neared the end of a long line of cars. Metal shone in the moonlight.

As he approached the next car, he spotted a figure standing on the border of his lot. The sight caught him off guard, and his heart leapt into his throat. The hairs on his arms and back stood at attention. The man wore a suit, but his features weren't discernable. He stayed in the shadows, away from any light, and he stared directly at Dex.

"Can I help you?" Dex asked.

The man continued staring.

"We're closed!" Dex announced, but the man made no move to leave. His appearance and unwillingness to communicate were unnerving.

"Sanders!" John called from the other end of the lot. "You finished on your side?"

Dex's eyes were locked on the dark man, and he didn't pay attention to John's question. Two flashes of silver sparkled where the man's eyes should be. Like stars, they flashed and disappeared in a split second.

"Dex!" John called again.

Dex snapped his head around. "Yeah! I got it!" He waved to John.

"All right! I'm outta here! See you tomorrow!" John waved and walked away.

Dex turned back to the dark man. "Can I help—"

The man was gone. No one stood at the border. Either the man had disappeared, or Dex was going crazy.

DEX TOOK A DEEP BREATH, closed his eyes, and pushed the air out, releasing the day's tension. He turned the knob and entered his home.

"Hello?" he called out.

Thumping and running came from the floor above, and his wife called out, "Noah and Jacob. What did I say?"

Dex walked to the kitchen counter and took his ball cap off. He emptied his pockets of his wallet, change, and a pen, placed them inside his hat, and set it down. He sifted through the mail and held up a small box with a perplexed expression. It was addressed to him but had no return address. He held on to it, walked to the fridge, grabbed a water bottle, and took a drink.

"Ahh!" Reagan let out a tiny squawk as she turned the corner and saw Dex. She placed a hand to her chest. "You scared me. I didn't know you were home."

"You didn't hear me come in? I called to you."

"No. I can't hear a thing over your boys." She rolled her eyes.

"Driving you crazy?"

"Yes. All day, they've nitpicked at each other. Now I'm trying to get them into bed, and they're bouncing off the walls. You need to deal with them."

Laughter erupted from upstairs.

Dex took two steps toward the staircase and bellowed, "Boys. You'd better get to bed!"

"Oh yeah, that'll do it," she mocked.

"I'll go get them." He smiled.

"How was your day? Any sales?" The drop in her voice was familiar. It was an anxious tone struggling to muster up any hope.

"Not good." Dex shook his head. "I didn't talk to anyone the entire day. Not one person came in. Well, that's not true. There was one guy at the end, but I must have scared him away."

"What are we going to do? I hate this job," she said.

Dex slumped. "I know. I do too. It's just temporary until I find a better one."

"It's been two years now and four different jobs."

He'd walked away from a well-paid career surveying CATV and fiber optics construction. It took him all over the country and away from his family for weeks at a time. Every three weeks, he came home, only to have to pack up and leave again four days later. It took a toll on them all. Dex made a drastic choice to leave his career, feeling confident he'd find a better job locally. He didn't expect as much struggle as it had turned out.

He softened his eyes, leaned over, and kissed her forehead. "It's going to be okay. I promise."

Looking down, she nodded.

He turned and marched up the stairs, purposely stomping to tease his boys.

"Dad's comin'! You two had better be in bed by the time I get there!"

"Ahhh!" Noah and Jacob squealed. Panicked giggles sounded as they scampered for their bedroom.

Dex clomped his feet down the hall and pounded the walls with his fists.

"I'm getting closer."

The boys jumped into their beds.

"You'd better be lying down, with your covers pulled up to your necks and your eyes closed."

Their giggles escalated, and Dex stepped into their room.

"And lights had better be out!"

The two boys lifted their shocked faces. Their bedroom light was still on. Dex growled, then he flashed them a large grin.

Relieved, they both cried with excitement, "Daddy!"

"Hi, guys. Are you two giving Mom trouble?"

"No." Jacob was six years old. Lying on the bottom bunk, he defended their actions. "Noah kept tickling me and wouldn't let me get to bed!"

"He wouldn't? *Unbelievable*," Dex said, gasping in mock horror.

"Nuh-uh!" Noah, who was eight, cried from the top bunk. "That's not true. You were splashing water on me in the bathroom."

"All right, guys, that's enough. You both know better. When Mom tells you to get ready for bed, you do it. Understand?"

They both nodded.

"Did you brush your teeth?"

"Yes! See?" Noah gave a wide, toothy grin, and Dex inspected them.

"Well, you brushed a couple of them."

"No, I brushed them all."

"I did, Dad!" Jacob said, and Dex looked at his.

"Between the two of you, at least five teeth got brushed," Dex joked. "I hope you used toothpaste this time."

"We did," Noah said, then he frowned. "Dad, why are you always working?"

"I don't know. There are people in this world who say if you want a house, food, and clothes, then you have to give them money. And then they want you to work a job to get that money," Dex mocked.

"That's stupid," Jacob said.

"That's what I said," Dex said with a grim, exasperated roll of his eyes. "Now, it's late, boys. Time to get to sleep, okay?"

He gave them each a kiss, told them he loved them, turned the light out, and exited. Dex couldn't blame them for missing their daddy. He'd put his boys through a lot during the time he spent working out of state. Dex missed Jacob's first baseball hit in Little League, Noah's first successful basket in a game, and hundreds of other undiscovered moments.

Dex walked to his and Reagan's bedroom, and she met him at the doorway.

"You got them down?"

"Yes," he said.

"Thanks." She fell into his arms, hugging him and lightly pecking his lips.

"Anything else go on today?" Dex asked.

"No." She shook her head. "Just a million texts from my sister. She broke up with her boyfriend."

He raised his eyebrows. "Mister Wonderful?"

"Yeah." She chuckled. "I'm glad she finally came to her senses."

"Maybe number fifty-six will be the lucky one," Dex said.

"Doubt it." Reagan sighed.

She moved to the bathroom and began to wash her face as he plopped down on their bed and glanced at the package in his hand. He'd forgotten all about it. He tried to open it, but it was taped with several layers, making it impossible to get through with his fingers. Surrendering, he set it on the nightstand behind the lamp.

A dog's barking echoed from outside, and it went on for several minutes until he asked Reagan, "Is that the Chamberlains' dog?"

"Yes. He's been doing it off and on all day. I went over there, but no one answered, and the dog's bowl was empty, so I fed him."

"With what?"

"Their back door was open. I found his food and poured him some. I gave him water too," Reagan said.

Dex scrunched his face. "That's weird. I haven't seen them for a couple of days. Did they go on vacation?"

"If they did, they didn't tell anyone. Usually if they're gone, they ask us to watch Scruffy and gather their mail."

"And they left their house unlocked? Really strange. That's not like Wes."

"You also got something in the mail. Did you open it?" Reagan asked.

"The box? No. I need a knife to open it, and I'm too lazy to go down and get one."

"Maybe it's that million dollars we're waiting for," she grumbled.

"I'm sure that's it. It's probably some promotional deal. Inside will be a fantastic offer saying we're approved for a giant loan or credit card, or maybe we can lease a new car for one-ninety-nine a month. That's my favorite."

"I'll take the loan," she said, walking over to him, and took a swig from his water bottle.

"Yeah, if we can pay it back," he said.

She frowned, and he winked.

"Are you coming to bed?" he asked her.

"Yes. I'm worn out. I'll probably read for a bit first," Reagan said.

"Which means you'll read for five minutes." Dex chuckled.

"Are *you* coming to bed?"

"Not yet. I need to decompress. I'm going to go work on my best-seller."

"Get on that, would ya?" She grinned.

They small talked for a few minutes, then he tucked her in, kissed her, and left the room. Dex entered the office, next to the boys' room, and began working on his latest novel. He was a writer at heart, yet despite the many attempts, he was still unpublished.

It was his escape as much as it was his therapy. He found that when he wrote dialogue, characters, and plot, it helped him deal with his own issues.

He sat at his desk and wrote for over an hour nonstop. He was on a roll until he finished a chapter. He was stumped on how to start the next one, and drowsiness overtook him. He planted his elbow on the desk and propped his jaw up with his hand, studying the text he'd just written. He soon closed his eyes and slumped over in sleep.

AUTHOR NOTES: *Thank you for jumping on this locomotive with me. I promise to run at a high rate of speed until the end. When I came up with this idea, I was working as a car salesman for Lincoln and Mercury vehicles. Therefore, our main protagonist, Dex, is a car salesman, and like him, I was between jobs. The worst day I had is described in the first chapter. I worked from start to close without one customer coming in. Thankfully, those days are long gone now. After writing my coming-of-age thriller,* The Other Side of Elsewhere, *I was excited to dive into something this fast-moving that carried a lot of teeth.*

Chapter 2: Pointing the Finger

They found me.

Wes Chamberlain stared at the text on his phone, and his mouth went dry. He'd spent the last ten years preparing for a moment like this, and he asked himself if he was up to it. He wasn't so sure.

Marcus, where are you, Wes typed back.

In my office. I stayed late to finish a project, when I heard gunshots from the first floor.

Stay put. I'm on my way.

Dear god, hurry! They're on the stairs!

Wes wracked his brain, wondering who he had in the area who could get to Marcus more quickly. Quinn was more than an hour away, and Badger was busy scoping out a new safe house. "Shit."

Wes was flying down the freeway in a matter of minutes, pushing his BMW to its limits. He kept his eyes out for cops while weaving in and out of cars. Fortunately, the traffic was light, and he screeched to a halt in front of the office building in under twenty minutes. Wes half expected to see the place swarming with *them*, but no one was in sight. Minimal lights glowed throughout the structure. He checked the ammo in his clip, nearly dropping it from his shaking hands, then he slammed it back into the butt of his gun. He stuffed the pistol into the back of his pants and trotted to the entrance. The doors weren't locked, and he entered.

The security desk appeared empty, and then Wes saw the blood. There was a puddle of crimson on the tile, and a smeared trail ran to an unmoving body. It was a male wearing a black-and-blue uniform, and he was lying facedown. Wes withdrew his gun and ran to the elevators. He pushed the number three, which held a bloody fingerprint.

The doors opened on the third floor, and Wes exited while aiming his gun. Simon and Simon Advertising was in room 312, and he found it quickly. He cautiously entered. The office space was dimly lit, as only the security lights were on. Wes walked among the cubicles. So far, no blood or bodies. Each one was empty until he came to the one that carried the nameplate of Marcus Reed. The back of Marcus's head stood above the partition. Something wasn't right. His head was shuddering, as if he was sitting in an electric chair set to full blast.

"Marcus?" Wes stepped to the opening of his cubicle.

Marcus didn't turn. Not right away. His entire body was quaking in the clutches of something unseen. After Wes called his name three times, Marcus slowly turned in his chair to face him.

Wes stepped back in horror. He'd heard stories of this happening, but he'd never seen it in person. Such an inhuman, abhorrent act couldn't be described. Marcus looked as if he were having a seizure of immeasurable intensity, and his face was a shade of blue. Blood ran from both ears down his neck, and something black hung from his nose. It looked like a slug about two inches long. It hung for a moment, quivering back and forth with the rhythm of his shaking body, then it got sucked back up into his nostril and was gone. Marcus's mouth hung slightly open with a marginal smile, blood dangled from his lip, and his eyes... Oh Lord, his eyes were completely covered in a skin of bright silver.

"Marcus?" he asked again, but he knew it was fruitless. Marcus was gone.

Wes raised his gun and pointed it at Marcus's head. He had to put him out of his misery. His stomach twisted like a taffy machine. He *wanted* to end his pain, but how could he? It was his friend's face. The

Marcus-thing made a gurgling sound, which soon turned into a giggle. Was it laughing? A cold chill passed through Wes like a ghost.

Wes couldn't pull the trigger. He put his gun away and turned to leave, when something smacked into the side of his neck. It felt like a punch, and his scream was caught in his throat. A substance invaded his body, and it spread through his veins like a shot of morphine. A tall man with silver hair stood over him, pointing a gun, and then Wes blacked out.

DR. H FROWNED AS HE stared at the man who sat tied to a metal chair. Wes was his captive, and he wasn't giving up any information. The prisoner was bent in half. A string of blood ran from his bottom lip to the floor. He would be lying flat if the straps of the chair weren't holding him in, and Wes gasped for air as if he had run a marathon. One bold light illuminated him in the otherwise-dark room. The walls were made of cinder block, and the room held no furniture except for the metal chair.

Dr. H's eyebrows crinkled, and he glanced at Z, who wiped blood from his knuckles. Z was Doctor H's right-hand man. He was muscular, stood at a height of six feet two, and carried a face carved out of stone. The buzz cut of silver hair on top of his head did not indicate his actual age of thirty-eight.

Z turned to H and shook his head.

Dr. H crouched in front of his victim at eye level, but Wes kept his gaze down.

"Poor Wes Chamberlain. It didn't have to come to this." Dr. H's voice was soft. His eyes wandered across Wes's body, looking at the bloody puncture holes in his hands and arms. "We have your wife in the next room. She's strapped in a similar chair. I guess it's her turn."

Wes lifted his head as if fifty pounds of weight sat on top. One eye was swollen shut and purple, and the other eye was large and white. His face was a mangled mess of bruises and bumps. Through trembled lips, he spoke. "Don't touch my wife."

"Well, I don't want to. I really don't. Z's knuckles need ice and rest. But we need answers." Dr. H chuckled nonchalantly.

"I'm… going… to kill you. All… of you *bastards*," Wes panted.

Dr. H nodded. "I understand."

The doctor lifted an iPad for Wes to view the screen, and he tapped a button. A live image of his wife popped into view. She sat in a dark room in a metal chair, blindfolded. Her body shook, and tears streaked her cheeks.

Wes's entire body tensed, and he pressed against his bonds. He sank back in his chair and cried.

"You've been through a lot these past three days. Z has beaten you, run electric shocks through your body, and given you all manner of torture. I mean, look at your body. You can't take any more. Now, Wes, we are about to do the same to this sweet, innocent lady of yours. She has such impeccable, delicate skin. It's a shame. Why would you do this to her?"

Wes glared at him.

"A name, Wes. We just need a name. One name. As easy as that, and she doesn't have to go through the same pain."

Dr. H kept silent as he watched Wes process his thoughts. After a minute, without meeting his eyes, Wes mumbled, "Dex."

"What was that?" Dr. H asked. "Dex? Dex who?"

"Sanders."

AUTHOR NOTES: *This first scene was the last thing I wrote in this novel. I felt like Wes needed a little extra, and the story deserved more impact earlier on. It's very common to rewrite the first couple of chapters after finishing the whole story because you know your characters better now. Not to mention, the plot can change what should happen in the beginning.*

Chapter 3: The Abduction

Three black SUVs drove down the street and stopped outside Dex's home. Z stepped out of the front seat, wearing a T-shirt, jeans, and a leather jacket. He eyed the area warily. The night was quiet, and the street was empty.

Five men emptied the vehicles, armed with guns and dressed in dark military garb. They marched to the front door, and Z stared at the doorknob and dead bolt with intensity. His eyes glowed a bright silver, and he opened his mouth, and an inhuman sound escaped. It was a sharp sound but not loud enough to wake anyone.

The door handle and lock shimmered, mechanisms inside blew apart, and a puff of metallic dust blew out from the keyhole.

Z glanced at his men. They appeared set and ready. He pushed the door open.

They knew their places. Two men trotted quietly to the boys' room, two stayed at the foot of the stairs as backup, and Z and the final man approached Dex and Reagan's room.

Z's eyes adjusted to the dark quickly. He stepped to the couple's bed, and his eyes widened. Reagan was curled up, sleeping, facing him, but the other side of the bed was empty. Dex was gone.

Z stepped back, and the floor creaked. Reagan's eyes fluttered open. Z stared at her as she gained focus.

She shot up in bed and screamed, "Dex—"

Z aimed his pistol and shot a tranquilizer dart into her neck. Her eyes widened. She clutched her throat and moved her lips to talk, fighting to keep conscious, but the venom was too strong. She fell back onto the bed, unconscious once more.

HEAD SPINNING AND VISION blurred, Dex leaped out of his chair at the sound of Reagan's scream. He ran out of the office and into two men standing outside Noah and Jacob's room. The guys shared quick looks of surprise.

One man lifted his pistol to shoot, but Dex's instincts were quick. Dex lifted his left arm and smashed it against the man's gun arm and shot a front kick into the man's gut, doubling him over.

Dex twisted to the second man, smacking his rising gun arm away, and shot a side kick to his chest. The man crashed into the wall. Dex turned back to the first man with a left hook to his jaw followed by a right uppercut punch. The hit rocketed the stranger off his feet.

Noah and Jacob sat up straight, screams caught in their throats.

"Noah! Jacob!" Dex ran into their room.

Those were the only words Dex got out. A fist hammered into his solar plexus like a piston, all air escaped, and his knees buckled.

A million thoughts flooded his head: his boys, Reagan. *What did they do to her? What will they do to my boys? Who are these people, and what do they want?*

Two more men joined the first, and each pummeled Dex with punches and kicks. He was going down, and it terrified him. His family needed him. He couldn't fail them.

Dex's arms were grasped tight in their hands, and he was on his knees. He drew upon a newfound strength, a final desperate act to save his family, and stood up. He pushed his body against the two men behind him, slamming them against the wall. He jabbed his elbows backward into any body part he could reach with as much force as he could muster.

He snapped a front kick to the jaw of the man in front of him and heard his teeth crack, and blood flew.

"Reagan!" he screamed, and then he felt a punch to his neck. His hand immediately flew to the spot and found something sticking out of his skin. He turned and saw a monolith of a man with silver hair and a stone face. He pointed a gun at Dex. Words froze in Dex's throat, and his mind spun. He turned to his boys with tears in his eyes and toppled.

Noah cried, and Jacob hyperventilated. The silver-haired man stepped in front of Dex and raised his pistol. Dex reached for him, but he was three feet away.

He heard the man say, "Nighty night, boys."

Then Dex lost consciousness.

AUTHOR NOTES: *I've always wondered what it would be like if my house were broken into while my family and I were asleep. It's a terrifying thought. What may be more horrifying than that is what happens after they take you to another location.*

Chapter 4: A Strange New Place

Dex pulled his eyelids open. He was lying on cold concrete, staring at the ceiling. His entire body ached, and he shivered. He blinked several times to adjust his vision. His mouth was dry, and as he rolled to his side, he felt more aches and pains throughout his body. He took in his dismal surroundings. Everything was gray. He sat in a small, concrete room with cinder block walls. The room was empty except for a chair.

A man in a long white coat sat in that chair, smiling at him. Three men scowled in the background. One of them was large in stature with silver hair and kept his arms folded. Dex briefly remembered this man shooting him.

"Good morning, Mr. Sanders," the man in the chair said. His voice was smooth, almost comforting. "How are you feeling?"

"Shitty."

Too weak to stand, Dex sat up. An image of his wife and kids flashed in his brain.

"My family! Where are they?"

"They're fine, Mr. Sanders. I assure you."

He shook his head slowly. Rage boiling, Dex snarled. "Where are they? What the hell is going on?"

The man in the white coat put out a soft hand and made a patting motion. "Please. I know you have a lot of questions, and they will all be answered. Right now, your family is completely fine and safe, and they will remain that way if you answer my questions honestly."

"What the hell does that mean?" Dex snapped.

"I think it's quite clear." The man shrugged. "You give us what we want, and you and your family go free. I'm not a bad man, you see. I want the best for everyone. Unfortunately, it never goes that way. People are always so uncooperative. That is why I have Z."

He motioned to the silver-haired man.

"He's a specialist in pulling information out of subjects like you. I really am against his tactics." The man shuddered. "But I can't refute his results. If I need to use him, I won't hesitate. So it is in both of our interests for you to answer honestly."

Dex looked at the ground as thoughts swam in his head. He searched his memory for any reason why he'd be put in this situation. He tracked recent days back to months and years, but nothing came to mind.

He looked at the white-coated man, narrowed his eyes, and spoke. "I want a lawyer."

The man in the chair smiled, and the others broke out in laughter.

"Mr. Sanders. A lawyer is not going to help you here. We are not the police. We are not the FBI or even the CIA. One could say we're enemies to those institutions, and we are not held by the same rules. In fact, there are no rules here. Nothing can save you but telling the truth. It's that simple."

Fear bubbled in Dex's stomach, and a chill ran through his body. His gut churned and warned him of potential vomiting.

"Shall we get started?" The stranger grinned. "I haven't properly introduced myself. I am Doctor H."

"H?" Dex guffawed then nodded to Z. "And Z? Who are the other two guys? B and C? If everyone is a letter, does that mean you have twenty-two other men in your outfit?" Dex chuckled, and Dr. H's smile vanished.

"Let's get to the questions, shall we?" Dr. H said.

"Shoot. Let's get me and my family out of here."

"We are recording this session. We need names, Mr. Sanders, of your superiors and where we can find them. It's that simple," Dr. H said.

Dex scrunched his face. "Superiors? Like my boss at work? I don't understand."

Frustrated, Dr. H sighed. "Let's not play around. I have no patience. Don't make Z break your fingers."

Dex glanced at Z and his monstrous arms and gigantic hands. He was easily twice his size. Dex gulped in fear, not because he *wouldn't* answer their questions, but because he *couldn't.*

"You have to give me something more. I really don't know what you're asking me. My superiors to what?"

Z gave Dr. H a frustrated look.

"We know who you are," Dr. H continued. "We know the group you belong to. Not your job at the car lot, not your volunteer work at the church or anything of the sort. It's your other life. The one you don't want anyone to know about. Perhaps your wife and kids don't even know. I understand that, and it's okay. I can keep a secret too. I won't tell them. You just need to tell me what I need to know, and then I'll let you all go."

"Right." Dex nodded. "You nailed it on the head. I think there has been a big misunderstanding. You have the wrong guy."

One of the men behind Dr. H stepped out front, withdrew a pistol, and shot three times. The bullets hit the concrete inches from Dex, spitting up shrapnel. Dex's heart leapt into his throat, and he jumped back and felt a sudden urge to pee and shit at the same time.

"I told you not to play games with me. Why does everyone choose to play games?" Dr. H's face reddened. He stood up and pointed at Dex, enraged. "*Enough!*"

"Really." Dex put his hands out. "I have no idea what you're talking about. Honest. I don't want to be hurt. I don't want to die, and I don't want my family hurt or killed. There is nothing that important to die for. You have to believe me."

"You will want to die," Dr. H hissed. "After we're through with you, you will be begging us for the sweet relief of death."

Dr. H turned and looked at his men. They stepped out of the shadows. Dex saw the fresh bruises on their faces. One of the men's lips were swollen. Dex was sure he was the one he'd kicked in the jaw.

"These two have been begging me to let them get a crack at you. I think I'll give them that." Dr. H turned to them. "Five minutes. No more."

Dr. H left the room, and the two men advanced on Dex while Z stood back. Dex protected his face and body as best as he could, but the punches and kicks did their damage. His kidneys, ribs, hands, gut, face, and head received several blows. It felt like the punishment would never end. Even after it was through, it felt like it was still happening. He lay curled up, bleeding and panting. He closed his eyes and soon blacked out.

AUTHOR NOTES: *Dex is about to wake up to a nightmare. Having men break into his house the previous night and take him and his family captive probably seems like a bad dream, but Dex is about to realize how real it all is.*

Chapter 5: The Interrogation

Dex opened his eyes to a different room. All four walls were covered in white subway tile, and in the far corner stood a metal table with an array of surgical tools. His body clenched at the sight. He tried to move his hand, but it was tied down. So was his other arm and both legs.

He was lying on a gurney that might as well have been a flat board.

His face and body ached from the earlier beating. He knew one of the men wanted to smash his teeth in, but Z had stopped him before he could.

While he slept, he'd dreamt of his family and pictured them being questioned and tortured. He saw his kids crying. He heard Noah cry, "Where is my daddy?" Jacob was curled into a ball, sobbing.

A door opened, snapping Dex out of his thoughts. Dr. H stepped into view. He placed a chair in front of Dex. Dr. H held an iPad as he sat down.

"Good afternoon, Mr. Sanders," Dr. H said.

"Is it?" Dex grumbled.

"It's all perspective. How are you feeling?"

"Where is my family?"

"I understand." Dr. H nodded. "You're concerned, but you know the conditions."

Dex's jaw tightened.

"I have more questions for you, Mr. Sanders. I want to get to know you better, so we're going to start from the beginning."

Dex gave a burning stare at Dr. H's fake smile.

"You were born to June and Harold Sanders on April fourth, 1980. Eight months later, you ran a high fever that couldn't be controlled, and you were placed in the hospital. Your parents nearly lost you."

Dex stared at him blankly.

"Are you aware of that? Did your parents ever tell you?" Dr. H asked.

Dex stayed quiet.

"I asked you a question, Mr. Sanders."

Still nothing.

"Fine." Dr. H's voice was sharp. "Let's move forward. You attended Clairmont Elementary School from second grade to fifth grade. Do you recall that time?"

Dex's expression was unchanged.

"Are we going to have difficulty with you today? I really thought you'd be more cooperative."

"I. Want. To. See. My. Family. You can get your gorillas to beat me again, torture me, whatever you want, but it's only going to get you further from my cooperation. *Understand?*"

Dr. H rolled his eyes. "Fine. I'll let you see your family."

A ping of excitement shot through Dex.

"I will do this for you, but you must answer my questions. Understood?"

"Yes." Dex's heart felt ready to burst.

The doctor tapped several times on his iPad then turned it to face Dex. Across the screen was a view of the white room his family resided in. From an overhead view, he saw Reagan huddled with his two boys, her back propped up against the wall. There were no beds, pillows, or blankets. Not even a place for them to sit.

Dex swallowed hard. He didn't want Dr. H to see his tears, but he couldn't help the fluid that ran from his right eye and down his cheek. He looked for movement and saw it in all three of them. They were alive, thank God. He squinted, looking closer, and noticed Jacob's body quivering.

"Bastards."

Dr. H pulled the iPad back and turned it away.

"You fucking animals. They don't have *anything.* They're practically naked, and you couldn't even give them a blanket? They're shivering and cold. Have they even eaten? Are you feeding them? What the hell's going on here, H?"

"We're not barbarians." Dr. H motioned with his eyes to someone behind Dex. "We're feeding them."

"They need blankets, pillows, and mattresses too. Give them a damn room." Dex's body boiled with rage. "And you'd better be feeding them." His face shook, and more tears leaked.

"I'll do what I can for their comfort," Dr. H said.

"You'd better do more than that. I'm not talking until they're taken care of."

"Perhaps you'd rather see them tied up. Electrocuted. My gorillas can work them over. They have no scruples." Dr. H's face remained expressionless. "Must I remind you of the zero legs you have to stand on here?"

"It's information in *my* head you need," Dex growled through gritted teeth. "Do I need to remind you of that?"

"I can get that information from someone else. Your life will be forfeit, of course."

"Go ahead," Dex challenged. "I'm not playing by your games. You want information, you will take care of my family and promise me you won't hurt them. Is that *understood*?"

Dr. H looked at Dex for several moments then raised his eyebrows.

"I think we started off on the wrong foot." His eyes moved to the man behind Dex again. "Take his family some blankets, pillows, and food, please."

Dex heard the door behind him open and close.

"Compromise, Mr. Sanders. I'm not without it. We can work together to get each other what we want."

Dex took in deep breaths to settle his wired body.

"May we start again?" Dr. H asked.

Dex nodded.

DR. H RESITUATED HIMSELF in his metal chair and eyed Dex carefully. He shifted his eyes to the iPad, tapped a couple of buttons, and then looked at Dex again.

"Resuming, I had previously asked you about Clairmont Elementary. Do you remember your years there?"

"Most of it, I guess," Dex said.

"In fourth grade, you made friends with Billy Gordan."

Dex closed his eyes and sifted through his memory.

"Billy was my best friend. We were inseparable. What does that have to do with anything?"

"It may have to do with everything. Then again, it may have nothing to do with anything. I'm trying to jog your memories. Please be as open as possible and answer honestly. This was our deal."

Dex nodded. "We were the class clowns, you know," he continued. "Every day, it was our mission to make our classroom laugh, and nothing was off limits. Sometimes it got us into real trouble, and our teacher held us back from recess. That was fine with us as long as we were together. So we'd be stuck in the classroom, bouncing jokes off each other and making fun of our teacher, principal, other kids, and such. Like I said, we were two peas in a pod, as they say. Partners in crime right to the very end."

Dex shifted his butt for a better position on the hard gurney.

"Our parents put us into karate lessons," Dex said, "and we felt invincible. We'd spend all day at school, practice our katas and techniques after school, and attend karate at night. Jack Bennett was our karate in-structor. Man, we wanted to be like him."

Dex's eyes glossed over as he reminisced. "I never had a better friend than Billy."

"What happened in junior high?" Dr. H asked. "It was November of your eighth-grade year."

Dex's body sank, and with a lump stuck in his throat, he shook his head.

"Take your time. It's okay," Dr. H said soothingly.

"I lost him. He went on vacation with his family. They were gone for weeks. Much longer than he said they would be. Drunk driver... *killed* them all in an accident. My mom and dad told me the news." Dex's body trembled as he relived it. He felt his chest close in.

"I couldn't believe it at first. I was numb. I kept expecting to see him the next day at school or at karate, but it was just an empty chair. He was... gone.

"They had funeral services for them," Dex continued, "but no view-ing. Their bodies weren't presentable. But I think that's why I had a hard time believing he was really gone. I was on auto mode for the rest of the year. I missed a lot of karate lessons, and I was dead silent in class. I'd lost my compadre. I felt their eyes. Everyone in my class stared at me. They were sad, too, but not just for the loss of Billy. They grieved the loss of me too." Dex swallowed hard. "*Wow*. I haven't thought about Billy in years."

Dr. H gave him a moment of silence then tapped a button on his iPad and continued the questionnaire.

"Two years later, you lost your own family," Dr. H said.

Dex squinted and clenched his jaw. "Man, is that all you care about? Bringing out all my traumatic events?"

"They shape us, Mr. Sanders, whether you care to admit it or not. They tell me who you are."

"If you already know about them, why bother to ask me?"

"I want to hear your words. Hear what you went through and how you felt. Trust me. It's important," Dr. H urged him.

Dex sighed. He planned to spit out short answers and move on. He was through with feeling the pain of his past.

"Yes. They died. A car accident like Billy's. Okay?"

Dr. H typed something into his iPad.

"Surprised I can even get into a car today. It's too much for a young child."

"You were their only child, correct?" Dr. H asked.

"Yes. And I certainly was alone after that." Dex stared at the ceiling.

"Your karate instructor, Jack Bennett, took you in. A father, of sorts."

"Yes. He was an extremely good man. He did the best he could. I learned everything I know from him. He taught me how to survive. We practiced karate and fighting techniques every waking minute, and then we started weapons training. Knives, nunchucks, the staff, swords, and guns. Man, he had every type of gun, and I got good with them."

"It explains how you took out several of my men the other night," Dr. H remarked.

"He trained me and put me into tournaments, and I won a lot of them. I haven't used it in years, but it sure came back when I needed it," Dex said.

"How was he with raising you?"

"He was single. He never had kids, so I don't blame him for not knowing how to deal with a child, let alone a teenager. I think he did good. He was strict. I don't know if that was the instructor or father in him, but he made sure I followed whatever rules he set out. I can say I was lucky to have two fathers. My original, of course, who was loving and caring and who'd do anything for me. And Jack, who stepped up to the plate, held me accountable, and formed me into the man I am today."

"What happened to Jack Bennett?" Dr. H asked.

More silence as Dex took a deep breath.

"He woke me up one night." Dex let out sigh. "I still remember the panicked look in his eyes. He said he had to go. He owed some gambling debts in California or some shit. I don't know. He had a girlfriend at the time, and he said she'd take care of me. I was seventeen. I didn't really need anyone to take care of me anymore, but I stayed with her awhile until I got onto my own two feet. She was a good gal."

"Gambling debts?" Dr. H questioned.

"That's what he told me, but I didn't believe him. I never saw him gamble. That doesn't mean he didn't, but as much time as he spent teaching karate and teaching me, I don't know where he found the time to gamble." He shook his head in disappointment. "I can't believe he just took off like that. Some freaking father he turned out to be." Dex gritted his teeth.

"What do you think he was really into? Why did he disappear?" Dr. H pressed.

"I don't know. I really don't. He just up and disappeared. What can I tell you?"

"The truth."

"Fuck you," Dex snapped. "What do you think I've been saying this whole time? I fuckin' opened my chest up like a can of beans, spilled everything onto the floor, and for what? *For what?*"

"Mr. Sanders," Dr. H said softly. "Of all the people and the father figures who failed you, the parents you lost, the best friend you lost, do you really want your children to grow up without *their* parents?"

Dex pressed at his bonds. He wanted to wrap his hands around the doctor's throat and squeeze the life out of him.

"I simply want the truth." Dr. H gestured with open hands. "If I don't get it from you, what do you think happens? I'm liable to just kill you and your wife and let your boys grow up like you did. Fatherless and motherless. What do you think about that?"

"I think I'm going to tear into your throat with my fingers, reach down your neck, and rip your beating heart out. What do you think about that?"

Dr. H shook his head and tutted. "Sounds a bit harsh. It doesn't have to come to that."

"I don't know what you want to know. Tell me what I'm supposed to tell you, and I'll tell you. Did I give someone a bad look one day? Forget to pay a debt? Sell you a bad car? *What?*"

Dr. H took in a deep breath and let it out. "We're done for today. We're not getting anywhere. I hope you ponder what we've talked about. Think about the consequences. I've been more than generous."

Dex huffed in protest.

Dr. H withdrew a small eye dropper, walked to Dex, and brought it down to his eyes to apply the mysterious liquid held within. Dex clenched his eyes shut and struggled against Dr. H, who pried his eyelids open with his other hand and dropped fluid into each eye.

He instinctively shut his eyes and screamed in pain. The intense stinging shot through his pupils like fire and sent shock waves through his entire body.

"Open your eyes. *Open, Mr. Sanders!*"

Dex shook his head, clenching his eyes and teeth.

"The pain will go away once you open your eyes," Dr. H announced.

Dex finally opened his eyes. The pain instantly disappeared.

"These drops are designed to hurt you if you close your eyes. Keep them closed for too long, and it can even cause blindness. We don't want you sleeping. We want you awake and thinking."

Dex stared up at him, forcing his eyelids to stay open.

"I want you to think about what we talked about. Think about your family. Think about your choices and consequences. After all, that's what life is. Choices and consequences. Choose your time and thoughts carefully. I'll return... sometime."

He smiled and walked away.

Dex couldn't hold his eyes open any longer. He shut them, felt fire, and instantly opened them again, his chest frantically pumping up and down.

AUTHOR NOTES: *In 1989, a movie with Tom Selleck came out called* An Innocent Man. *The premise always intrigued me, and I wondered what would happen if the bad guys kidnapped the wrong guy, and he really doesn't know anything. The frightening thought is, what will they do to you and your family once they find out you are innocent, and they have no use for you?*

Chapter 6: He's Yours

Two hours passed by like an eternity. Dex lay on the gurney, occasionally fighting against his restraints but to no avail. He glared at the ugly ceiling made up of porous tiles spotted with stains. He forced his eyes to stay open for as long as he could. When his lids closed, the pain felt like broken glass was pressing against his pupils.

He memorized every inch of the disgusting ceiling. The yellow stains appeared like bladder accidents, and he couldn't understand them. *Was someone peeing on the ceiling?* It didn't take him long to deduce the cause was oxidation from water damage.

Those questions ate up about sixteen minutes of time, and he had hours to go.

He could keep his eyes open for three minutes at a time before needing to close them again. He shut his lids, felt the excruciating pain, and opened them again.

Thoughts of his family drifted in. Pictures of them in the lonely, cold room drove him crazy. Did the bad men hold their promise? Did they give them blankets, food, and water? Beds to sleep on?

What was his family thinking? They must be so scared, so *frightened*. He was concerned about Jacob. Jacob internalized traumatic situations and amplified them. Noah was the opposite. He stayed resilient in troubled or scary times.

There was a moment last summer while they were camping. They'd found a remote spot all alone in the canyon and planted their tent, built a fire, roasted hot dogs and s'mores—the whole works.

It was late at night when Noah tripped over a rock and instinctively put his hand out for support and planted it straight into the hot coals of the fire. "*Ahhh!*"

Dex would never forget his scream or the look of agony and terror on Noah's face. Dex and Reagan leapt into action, cooling it off with water and wrapping it in a towel, but it was clear he needed medical attention.

As Dex approached their car, his stomach churned as he saw the dim light draining from his headlights. *I left them on!*

He put the key in the ignition and turned it. The engine groaned then gave out with a loud clicking sound. Horror struck him but not like it did Jacob.

Dex and Reagan didn't give up hope. They couldn't. They were the parents. Dex opened the hood while Reagan tried to find a signal on her phone, but Jacob's face was panic frozen.

"What are we going to do?" Jacob cried.

"Honey, we'll find a way." Dex remained calm and tried to spread it to Jacob, but it didn't take.

"How? The car is broken. It won't run. We need to get Noah to a hospital."

"Jacob, we've got this," Regan reassured him. "Don't worry."

Noah sat on the end of a log, shaking. Tears continued to roll, but his sobs were under control. Jacob stared at him like he was on the brink of death.

"Mom! We need to get him to a hospital," Jacob repeated.

"I know, honey. We're trying."

Jacob began pacing back and forth and fidgeting with his hands. Dex glanced at Jacob and saw true terror in his eyes.

Fortunately, a camper nearby heard their cries and trotted to their campsite. It was a father and his twelve-year-old son.

"What's wrong? Anything I can do to help?" the stranger asked.

Dex turned like he'd seen an angel drop from the sky.

"Yes." Dex trotted to him. "Yes, please, my boy tripped into the fire, and his hand got burned. We need to take him to the hospital, but my car won't start."

"Need a jump?"

Dex nodded.

The man was fast to bring his truck over, and he had his own jumper cables, and Dex's car started in no time. On their way down the mountain, it took Jacob a long time to calm down. Reagan talked calmly to him, asking him to breathe in deeply and slowly, and eventually got his panic attack under control.

Now, being taken away from home, separated from each other, and held prisoner in a room, Jacob had everything to fear and panic about.

Dex's heart swelled, and he cried. He cried for Jacob's suffering, for the fear his wife was experiencing, and how lost Noah must feel. *Will I see them again? Tuck them into bed and kiss them good night? Was that the last time I'll see them? Did I tell them I love them? I did, didn't I? Yes.* He was sure he did. *But was it enough?*

No! He wanted to see them again. He wanted to take them home, watch them go to school, take them on trips, watch them fall in love with girls, graduate school, and become young men. He wanted more laughter and intimate moments with his wife, more sad moments when they wondered how they'd get out of the financial mess they were in, and then the triumph of overcoming it.

His chest heaved from sobs, tears filling his eyes and running down his cheeks. He cried harder than he had in years. It went on for ten minutes or more, and then he realized the burning feeling was all but gone. It stung a little when he closed his eyes but not nearly as much. On a scale from one to ten, the pain was a three, maybe a two. The tears had either flushed out the fluid Dr. H gave him or neutralized its strength.

He thought of his family again. He wanted all those things. He wanted them back, alive and well.

DR. H ENTERED HIS OFFICE, where Z sat behind his desk, cleaning a pistol. All parts of the gun were displayed on a cloth. Z turned his eyes to him. Exasperated, Dr. H shook his head.

"I'm getting nowhere," Dr. H said.

"That's no surprise. You know what I'd do." Z glanced at his gun.

"Yes. You want bloodshed. You thirst for it like a vampire. You want to pummel and torture men to death. I don't understand your fascination."

"It's not a fascination. It gets results."

"I can't argue with that, but there is a process. Every answer, or nonanswer, every movement, roll of the eyes, snarl, smirk, smile, or fidget tells me something. There are certain reactions to questions that elicit certain responses, and he isn't responding in any way that leads me to believe he knows anything at all."

Dr. H sat in a chair across from Z.

"What are you saying?" Z's steel gaze challenged him.

"Wes Chamberlain. He gave you a wrong name. A dummy name."

"You question the information I got from Wes?" Z asked.

"*Yes.* Look at it. He gave you the name of his neighbor. *His neighbor?*" Dr. H's eyes widened. "The man with a wife, two kids, and a shitty salesman job? How does that even make sense? Two of our greatest enemies happen to live next door to each other, and one of them sells cars for a living?" Dr. H rubbed at his right temple.

Z stood up and marched to where Dr. H sat. H craned his head to look at him.

"I broke Wes. Like a wild stallion, and he vomited everything. He gave us more information than anyone ever has before," Z said.

"But still not the information we need. We don't know where they're hiding or who is leading them."

"*He is their leader.*" Z pointed outside the room, referring to Dex. "*He* is the key. We are close to ending this."

Dr. H sighed.

"It's time to put him in my hands. I will get the information out of him. He has a wife and children. He will break easier than you think. Easier than Wes."

"We'll see," H surrendered. "He is yours."

AUTHOR NOTES: *What if there were eye drops that your captor could drip into your eyes that would make it too painful to close them, and you had to keep them open? It was one of those crazy, dark ideas that crept into my head one day. You wouldn't be able to get sleep, and your eyeballs would dry out. Hmmm, let's see how Dex handles it, shall we?*

Chapter 7: Torture

Three men entered Dex's room to give him water and assist in relieving his bladder, which was ready to explode. He'd been holding back the urge to pee, but it was so painful he couldn't focus on anything else.

One man unstrapped his right hand while the other two stood back with guns aimed. "Don't make a mess. If you get pee everywhere, I'll wipe it up with your face," the man grumbled.

Dex was given a plastic vessel to pee in. He did his business for all to see. After peeing, he had three swallows of water before they took the bottle away, strapped him back to the gurney, and wheeled him out of the room. He stared at the lighted ceiling of the long hall and caught glimpses of closed doors. He tried to study his surroundings, but there was nothing distinctive he could make out. Nothing that told him where he was.

A door opened, and they pushed him into a dark, gray room. One dim light was on, and it spotlighted a metal chair in the far back but kept the rest of the room in shadows.

Two men unstrapped him while the third kept his distance and aimed his gun.

They led him to the chair, a bulky hunk of metal that looked like a mix between a medieval torture device and an electric chair. Leather straps hung open from the arms and legs. The men strapped Dex in without incident.

"More water?" Dex begged.

They stared at him without answer, but he could read their faces. They were hesitant to give him any.

"Just a bit more? Please?"

One man shrugged, opened the lid on the water bottle, and held it to his lips. A couple of ounces got in, and the rest went down his shirt.

The door opened, and Z marched in.

"Is the prisoner secure?" Z asked as he took his jacket off to reveal the tight gray T-shirt he wore underneath.

"Yes," the lead man answered Z. "He's secure. Where's Dr. H? Is he coming?"

"He'll be here." Z looked at the bottle in his hand. "Did you give him water?"

"A little." He nodded.

"No more," Z snarled.

Z approached Dex and ran his eyes up and down the entire length of his body. Dex stared back at him.

"You're going to talk today," Z said.

"I've been talking this whole time."

Z smirked and searched Dex's eyes long enough to make him uncomfortable.

A flash of silver crossed Z's eyes, like a second eyelid that came from the bottom of his eye to the top and back down. It was as quick as the blink of a regular eye, and Dex remembered the night at the car lot. The dark stranger had flashed the same silver eyes, but he didn't know what it meant.

"I want what's in there." Z tapped Dex's forehead. "You'll give it to me." He smiled deliciously.

The door opened again, and Dr. H entered. He carried a folding chair to Dex's side and sat down. He nodded to Z, and Z turned and stepped away.

"I see you got some sleep," Dr. H said.

"If you can call what I got sleep," Dex answered.

"The drops should last for ten hours. They seemed to lose their potency after two and a half with you. Maybe less." Dr. H raised his eyebrows.

"Did you check the expiration date?" Dex smirked.

"Mr. Sanders, I have given you every opportunity to reveal your plans to me, and the whereabouts of your group. I am done with pleasantries, and quite frankly, I'm exhausted with your sarcasm," he groused.

Plans? Dex thought. *Group? What group?*

"I don't know what your problem is, but I'm having a great time." Dex's sarcasm was his only defense. If he could piss them off, he would.

"I need to know more about Jack Bennett. I need to know where he is," Dr. H said.

Dex scrunched his face. "How the hell should I know? We talked about this yesterday. He left when I was seventeen. I never saw him again."

Dr. H turned to look at Z, and Z marched to Dex's left side. There was an opening in a portion of the chair exposing Dex's lower back, and Z pounded his right kidney with a punch. It felt like a horse kick, and he arched his back in pain.

"If you think that was painful," Z hissed, "you've got another think coming."

"I get it, Dex. I do," Dr. H said. "You're trying to protect them all. But right now, you should be thinking about your family. Do you think Bennett is concerned about you? How about the rest of your group? You've been here for how long? Where are they? Why haven't they come to rescue you if they care so much?"

Dex glared at Z and shifted his eyes to Dr. H.

"I don't know anything. *What* group are you talking about? If Jack Bennett was into something illegal or he's wronged you or owes you money, then your problem is with him. *Not me.* He never included me in anything. I was a *kid*. All he told me was that he owed some gambling debts. Is that what this is about?"

Z walked around and punched him in the other kidney.

He winced in pain, air escaped his lungs, and he felt dizzy. Dex snapped at Z. "*I'm serious.* I don't know anything. You have the wrong—"

Z's knuckles raked across his right cheek in a blur.

Z stepped back, rubbing his fist. Dex's cheek burned, and he felt swelling start, and blood filled his mouth.

Z grinned.

"It's only going to get worse," Dr. H said.

Dex wasn't sure how to convince them. He contemplated giving them a fake story, fake names, and a fake address, but he knew they wouldn't buy it.

"Look. I want to help you." He looked at both Z and Dr. H, hoping to connect with them so they would believe him. "I want my family back. I want to go home. I know what's at risk here. There is no reason for me to lie. It's just... I have no idea what you're talking about," he said with sincerity.

Z walked over to the wall next to him. There was a metal box on the wall, and he opened the small door of the console and turned a dial.

The electric current was instant and shot through Dex's entire body. The surge of power immobilized him. His body clenched. He couldn't move even if his bonds were released. His head craned back, and his teeth chattered.

Z turned the dial off, Dex was released from the electric grip, and he sank in his chair. The air smelled burnt, and drool dripped from Dex's lips.

Z approached him. "Cat still got your tongue?"

It took a moment for Dex to catch his breath. He finally lifted his head and spoke. "I am telling you the truth. The only truth there is."

Z stepped to the console again, and Dex gritted his teeth, shut his eyes, and prepared for a torture that no one could prep for. Z turned the dial and sent a current through him for double the time.

Once the electrocution was finished, Dex's body began to slip. Dex blinked in and out of consciousness. Z pulled Dex's body upright and slapped his face until his eyes fluttered open.

"Still with us?" Z asked.

Dex lifted his burning eyes to meet his. He truly hated this man. Dex was softhearted and lived his life trying to find the best in everyone. It was hard sometimes, but he believed there was generally something good in everyone. Hate was such a strong, powerful emotion, and he avoided it as much as possible. But looking up at this piece of shit in front of him, he could say, right down to the heart and bone, that he hated this man.

"Kinda smoky in here, isn't it?" Z chuckled as he waved phantom smoke from his nose. "It smells like burnt toast."

"Your body can't take any more of this, Dex. You must give us what we need," Dr. H urged him.

"How can I give you what I don't have?" Dex's voice cracked.

"This man"—Dr. H pointed at Z—"is a vile barbarian. I agree with you. He's insane, and he enjoys inflicting pain."

Z continued to smile.

"But Dex. He will not stop. He is an unchained beast, and there are only two things that will stop him. Either we get the information we need from you, or you die. Whichever comes first," H begged.

Dex chuckled painfully with a disturbed look of his own. "You two are really good at this good cop, bad cop routine. You know that?"

Z ran to him in a blur, and his iron fist shot out, hitting Dex's face on the left side of his nose. Dex's head snapped back against the metal chair and then sank cheek to chest. The blow knocked him out.

AUTHOR NOTES: *I went a little dark here. I wanted to explore various stages of what a man might go through as evil people try to get information out of him. I had originally written a number of scenes where Dex gets tortured, but in rereading it, I'd gone a bit strong. I scaled it back as I wanted to keep this more grounded in reality and follow what served the story and characters better. My wife doesn't like torture scenes. Who can blame her? I promise it's not too harsh, but what pops up in the metal torture chair may surprise you.*

Chapter 8: Crossing the Line

Dex slowly regained consciousness and felt the cold metal beneath him. He was still tied to that chair. He felt pain throughout his entire body, like someone had stripped him of every muscle and nerve, run them through a meat grinder, and reattached them. He heard a discussion taking place between Z and Dr. H. Their voices were low, but he could hear them. He kept his eyes closed, pretending to stay unconscious, and listened.

"Have they searched the place?" Dr. H asked.

"Yes. They haven't found a thing," Z replied.

"I told you we shouldn't have trusted Mr. Chamberlain's story."

"I'm not convinced yet. Something's at play here. I'll give you that. But Dex is with them. He is the key." Z sounded confident.

Chamberlain? Dex thought. *Wes? Are they talking about Wes?*

Dr. H asked, "Is everything set?"

"Yes. Let's get this done," Z answered.

Was Wes here? Did he lie to them? Did he point the finger at me? It was starting to make sense now. Anger flared up in his system and heated his body with rage. *How could Wes do this to me and my family?*

Dex opened his eyes and badly wanted to rub them, but his hands were still strapped to the chair. He felt an itch on his nose, too, and it was enough to drive him mad. He raised his head as Dr. H and Z crossed the room.

"You're back," Dr. H said, his half smile hiding something.

"Where's my family?" Dex asked.

"Always about the family." Z grinned and shook his head.

"Yes, *prick*. Where is my family?"

Z tensed and moved to hit Dex, but Dr. H held up a hand for him to stop.

"No, no, not again. We need him conscious," Dr. H said and moved his eyes to Dex. "I'm going to try one more time. This is your last chance. Tell us what you know."

Dex nodded. "And then we get to go? Me and my family? We won't be harmed?"

"Of course not." His smile might as well have been painted on. "There'd be no reason to harm you. You'd all be free to go. I am a man of my word."

"Okay," Dex surrendered. "It was a few years ago when we first learned of your kind."

Z and H perked up like animals who had finally found their prey.

"I didn't believe it at first, but they convinced me. I saw it for myself."

H and Z drew in closer.

"I saw your spaceship. Big silver saucer hovering above the ground, filled with green aliens. We know who you are, and we're going to kick your asses back to your home planet."

Dr. H snarled, and Z marched away and spit.

"Do you hate needles, Mr. Sanders?" Dr. H asked.

Dex gave him a quizzical look.

"Like a doctor's needle. A syringe," Dr. H said.

"What do you mean? What are you going to do?" Fear bubbled inside Dex.

"You see all the tiny holes in the chair you sit on?" Z tittered.

Dex lifted his arms as far as he could and saw tiny holes lining the metal. The pin-sized holes ran down the arms and legs of the chair, and he could only assume they ran along his back, too, and beneath his ass.

Z held something in his hand. It was a remote with buttons, and he pushed one.

A hundred needles protruded simultaneously into his arms, hands, legs, ankles, back, and butt and quickly retracted. A needle barely missed penetrating his groin, and he feared that if he shifted or moved, the needle would find it on its next strike.

"*Ahhh!*" His entire body arched away from the chair as far as he could. The sharp sting from each needle was indescribable. His body deflated. Although the wounds were no more than getting a doctor's shot, it was enough to draw blood. Crimson smeared across the metal.

"*Ha-ha-ha!*" Z chuckled heartily. "Fun little gadget. It's my favorite."

Dex's heart pumped rapidly. He didn't know how much more of this he could withstand. He wished he *did* know something. He'd tell them. No secret was worth the safety of his family. *Some spy I'd make,* he said to himself.

"I don't know what to tell you," Dex said, and he eyed Z and Dr. H earnestly.

"You do know if you don't tell us, you will die. We'll have no use for you," Z said.

"And how much use do you have of me if I *do* give you the answers you want?"

"We told you," Dr. H said. "You and your family will be set free. We can't allow you a phone or means to communicate with your group until we've annihilated them, of course, but after, your lives will be yours."

"And if you have the wrong guy, if I don't have the information, you'll kill us."

"Of course," Dr. H said nonchalantly with a shrug.

"Shit." Dex shook his head and bowed.

"Mr. Sanders?" Dr. H asked but Dex didn't respond. "*Mr. Sanders!*" Still nothing.

"*Dex!*" Z hollered, but Dex didn't raise his head or speak. Z pushed the button three times rapidly.

Dex's body shot up, arching away from the needles that punched in and out fast. Each time, they marked his body with new holes and widened existing ones.

Dex whimpered, and tears streamed down his cheeks.

"Are you not going to speak?" Dr. H asked.

Dex kept his gaze on the ground and his lips closed.

Dr. H gave Z a final look, and Z nodded.

"This is your last hope, Mr. Sanders. One more chance to answer."

Z pressed different buttons on the remote, and Dex's chair spun one hundred eighty degrees on a mechanism. The cinder block wall in front of him slid to the side and revealed an entirely glass wall. On the other side of the wall was a different room.

The room was identical to his—gray brick walls and empty of furniture except for a tall metal chair. It held a prisoner.

"*Reagan!*" Dex exclaimed.

His lovely wife, Reagan, was strapped to a chair just like his. In an instant, he knew the hell she was about to experience.

"Say hi to your sweetie." Z smirked.

"*Reagan! Reagaaan!*" Dex hollered.

Her head was down, and her long brunette hair dangled. She was out but began to stir. She raised her head, and once her eyes gained focus, they flew wide open.

"Reagan!" he cried.

She mouthed, "Dex."

She couldn't hear him, and he couldn't hear her. Their eyes transfixed on each other.

She was still in her nightshirt and bottoms and was barefooted. Dark rings cupped her bloodshot eyes, but from what Dex could see, there were no wounds or bruises.

Dex was still in a T-shirt and sweatpants. His face bulged with swollen muscles. One eye was purple and black, half-shut. His lips were wet with blood, and then her eyes moved to the blood spots on his arms and the ones that leaked through the cloth of his pants, and she gasped. Tears ran, and her body trembled.

Dex relaxed his face and pulled a slight smile in hopes of convincing her he was okay or at least not as bad as he looked.

"She's lovely, Sanders." H stepped next to him. "I'd hate to see her go through what you've been through."

Dex's body was in shock from his trauma, and he shook uncontrollably. He continued to stare at Reagan. His mind sought solutions and sifted through a million scenarios, and none of them worked. He fought against his restraints, but it was no use. He closed his eyes, took a deep breath, and centered his focus. The only tool he had was diplomacy.

"Mr. H." He wouldn't call him doctor. He was no *doctor*. "I understand what you're trying to do. I really do. I'm not sure what you're into or what this other group has on you, but I know if I were in *your* shoes, I wouldn't want to waste time barking up the wrong tree. And that's what you're doing here. You must see that. It's not embarrassing to admit it."

He remembered the conversation between Dr. H and Z as he awoke. Dr. H was convinced that Wes had misled them.

"I see doubt in your eyes. You don't believe I'm the right guy. You know there was a mistake. Please admit it and just let us go. We are harmless. I'm a car salesman and married with two kids. I wouldn't risk my life or theirs by getting mixed up into this dangerous game."

"Don't listen to this," Z warned Dr. H. "He's lying."

"*Am I?*" Dex snapped at Z. "Prove it. Strap me to a lie detector test. That's how you do it. Start there. Not with torture."

There was silence as Z and Dr. H stared at each other. Z shook his head slowly. Dr. H appeared to still have his doubts, and Z fought him against it.

Z turned to the glass window and looked at Reagan.

"Electrocution first?" Z asked.

"*Nooo!*" Dex yelled. "*Please.*"

Z pushed a button, and Reagan's body clenched and quaked.

"*Bastards! Stop! Stop!*"

Z stopped, and her body relaxed and sank.

"Please, please, please," he begged. "Not my wife. Not my kids. Torture me, kill me, whatever it takes, but we know nothing. I will die knowing nothing, and you will get nothing, or I can help you."

Dr. H tilted his head in interest. "Help us? In what way, Mr. Sanders?"

"It was Wes Chamberlain, my neighbor, right? He blamed me for this. He told you some lie about me. I overheard you telling Asshole here." He jerked his head at Z.

"And how do you propose to help us?" Dr. H asked.

"Let us go, and I'll find him. I know where he'd be. Let my wife and kids go free, and you can keep a leash on me until I find him and bring him to you. That's the deal. But my family stays unharmed. Forever."

Both Dr. H and Z chuckled.

"Nice try," Z said.

"Mr. Sanders," Dr. H's voice softened. "Wes Chamberlain is dead. His and his wife's bodies were dumped in a field nearby. They were in these same chairs last week. It didn't work out so well for them, and it's not working out well for you two either."

Dr. H turned to Z. "Kill them. All of them. He knows nothing."

"No. *No! You can't do this!* We're not a threat!" Dex pleaded.

"I'd love to," Z answered Dr. H, disregarding Dex's pleas.

"No, not you," Dr. H said. "Pick two of your best men to dispose of them. I need you for something else. We'll talk in my office."

"*Please! Hey!* I can still help. You've got to let me help!" Dex cried.

"What is it, Mr. Sanders? Do you have something to tell us or not?" Dr. H asked.

Dex's head spun, his heart pumped like a piston, and his stomach churned with nausea. "I-I don't know," he cried.

Dr. H shook his head. "Waste of time." He looked at Z with anger. "Waste of *time*," he growled and walked out.

Dex turned to Reagan, who hadn't taken her eyes off him. "I'm sorry," he mouthed. "So sorry. I love you."

She broke into sobs. "No, no," she mouthed.

Images ran through his mind in a matter of seconds. He saw Reagan when she was seventeen, wearing a short peach shirt and turning from him with a large smile. They'd met at a friend's party, and Dex couldn't keep his eyes off her.

His mind sifted through various memories of dates and high school dances. Clips of their marriage flew by along with Noah's birth, Noah taking his first steps, and then the birth of Jacob. He remembered helping Noah when he fell and scraped his knee. He saw snapshots of their vacation at Disneyland and how they'd run to every ride. Jacob came down with a severe case of the flu last year, and Dex recalled spending all night with him. Jacob lay on his chest while Dex rocked him in a chair and tried to cool his fever.

Is this my end? Is this my life flashing before my eyes?

"Tell the boys I love them," he said, hoping she could read his words.

"What?" she mouthed and shook her head.

He took a deep breath. "It's okay. It's okay. I love you all."

"I love you! I love you!" she yelled.

Dex kept his eyes locked with hers until Z slammed his head with a fist, and he sank in his chair, head spinning.

AUTHOR NOTES: *Where is your line that people shouldn't cross? The line that triggers your innermost strength and anger to make you fight for everything that's precious to you? I know where my line is. I'm an easygoing man. Most people who know me joke about how I never get mad at*

anything. Clearly, they haven't seen me at the moment someone has crossed my line. And people have.

Chapter 9: Escape

Dex's body was slumped in the chair. He kept his eyes closed and remained limp. He heard people enter the room, but he remained still.

"Why did Z knock him out?" a man with a deep voice complained. "Now we have to carry dead weight."

"What does it matter? We're just going to kill him," a man with a higher-pitched voice said.

"We won't do it in here. We'll take him into the room where his family is and kill them all in there. Just one mess to clean up. It's what we did the last time. Did you bring the plastic?"

"Yes."

"Good. We'll lay that down first."

Dex felt hands unbuckling his restraints. *Just keep still. Pretend to be dead,* he told himself. Dex's body tilted forward and was about to fall when he felt arms catch him. Dex contemplated taking the two men out right now. His hands and feet were free, and he could catch them by surprise.

"A little help here," the deep voice implored, and after a shuffle of feet, Dex felt two more hands lift him.

"We'd better cuff him," the other guy said.

Dex's hands sat in his lap. He felt metal rings clasp over his wrists.

Yes, he thought. They cuffed his wrists from the front instead of from behind. It gave Dex more leverage and an idea.

The two men dragged Dex out of the room and down the hall. They dragged him up two sets of stairs. His feet thumped against each step, and the edges scraped his heels. He suppressed the pain. They grunted as they pulled his dead weight. He heard one of them panting. *Good,* Dex thought. *I'm tiring them out.* They exited the stairwell and hauled him down another corridor. It didn't take long before they came to a stop. He heard the unlocking and opening of a door, and then he was pushed through.

"Dad!" Noah cried.

"Dex?" Reagan's voice was on the verge of panic.

Dex feared they might think he was dead.

He was thrown to the floor. He felt his kids immediately hug and press themselves against him and heard their sobs. Then he felt Reagan's hands caress his head. He couldn't imagine what he must look like to them. All the blood, punctured holes, and bruises would be a horrifying sight.

He heard the ruffle of a plastic sheet and then the squeaking sound of metal against metal. Dex wondered what that was. Sound suppressors, perhaps? The guards might be screwing them onto the ends of their barrels.

Dex's eyes drew open, and he looked at his family and gave them a wink. "It's going to be okay," he whispered.

Dex pulled away from his family, turned, and begged for mercy from the two men. "Please." One guard was a tall, broad-shouldered man. The other guy was a head shorter. Dex clasped his hands together as if in prayer. "Have mercy on us."

The larger man glanced at the other, who shook his head.

Dex shuffled closer to them on his knees, and they pointed their guns. Each had a silencer on his pistol. The tall guy stepped closer to Dex, while the short guy stayed on his left. The big one pointed his gun at Dex's head.

"I need you to get on the plastic." The deep voice belonged to the large one. He nodded to the sheet.

"Please. I have a family." Dex's eyes filled with tears. "You can just let us go. We won't say anything."

The big man rolled his eyes, the barrel of his gun moving off target slightly, and that was Dex's moment. He wasted no time.

He leaped to his feet and wrapped his handcuffed hands around the large man's wrists, and in one quick movement, he twisted, snapping the guard's wrist bones. He hyperextended his arm at the same time by pressing his forearm into the man's elbow, and the gun popped into the air. Dex let go of him and snatched the gun.

The big guy was turned now so that he was between the second guy and Dex. Shorty didn't have a shot. As a painful yell escaped the guard's lungs, Dex slammed his pistol into the man's throat and then pounded a side kick into his chest, knocking him into Shorty. The second guard stumbled away from his falling partner. Now off-balance, Shorty shot his gun off into the ceiling.

Dex fired two shots into the shorter man, one in his chest and one in his head. He quickly did the same to the larger guard. Blood fanned the floor.

Dex turned to his family. Each of their faces was wrinkled with shock and horror.

"Sorry you had to see that," Dex said. "But we can't waste time. We have to go!"

He rummaged through the guards' pockets for the key to his handcuffs.

"How... How did you do that?" Reagan shook her head in disbelief.

"I don't know." Dex shrugged. "Instinct, I guess. My boyhood training finally coming through."

He found the key and handed it to Reagan. She fumbled with it in shaky hands but eventually pushed the key into the lock and turned it, and Dex was free.

Dex gave each of them a quick hug and picked the pistol back up.

"All right. You guys ready?"

Still in astonishment, no one could answer, but Jacob and Reagan nodded. Noah remained frozen.

"Stick close to me. We need to find a way out, and we have to be very quiet. Can you guys do that?"

Reagan held the kids close to her as Dex opened the door carefully, aiming his gun at anything outside. The hall was empty. He motioned for them to follow.

With a brisk but cautious stride, Dex led them to the left. They passed two closed doors and reached the end of the hall. There were no windows, but there was a door to the stairwell. He opened it and stepped through.

DR. H SAT IN HIS OFFICE, and his eyes grew wide. He felt the deaths of Steve and Nick, the two guards they'd sent to kill Dex. Dr. H couldn't read their minds anymore. Their thoughts were empty. He sent out messages with his mind but got nothing back. He turned to Z, who wore a disturbed look. He'd felt it too. Dr. H was sure.

"I knew it," Z grumbled through gritted teeth.

Dr. H turned to the security monitors on his desk to see Dex and his family step out into a stairwell. "Send out the distress call."

DEX AND HIS FAMILY reached the bottom floor and stepped into an empty hall.

There was one door at the far end and three others that lined the corridor. After a quick inspection of each, he discovered two of them led to empty offices. The third held the torture room with the metal chair he'd just left. A shiver ran through his body. He trotted to the last door at the end of the hall and threw it open. Inside was another short hall. One side was lined with three windows covered by drapes. The hallway ended with another door. Above the door was a sign that read Utility Closet.

Dex approached the first window and pulled a corner of the drape away. All he saw was blackness except for a slight illumination, enough for him to determine that he was looking out into a vast space but nothing discernable. *Is it the outside?* It didn't feel like it.

He turned to Reagan, who wore a look of panic.

"Where do we go? How do we get out of here?" she muttered.

"I don't know." Dex shook his head.

Dex had woken up inside this building, but he did not know where they were. He had no idea how many floors the building held, and the absence of windows to view the outside further complicated his perception. "Let's go back!" he said.

Dex ran to the stairwell, and they hiked up to the next floor. Adrenalin pumped through his veins with such ferocity that it made his body numb to his wounds. *Just make it out alive,* he told himself. *I'll heal later.*

As they stepped onto the landing, the door opened, and two armed men stepped through. Without hesitation, Dex fired three shots into the first man. The second man shielded himself behind his comrade and fired blind shots, barely missing Dex and his family.

The guard pushed his dead coworker forward, and the body tumbled onto Dex, who grabbed him and pushed back. The guard pressed harder against the dead body, and Dex released his hold, causing the guard to stumble forward. Dex pushed the dead body aside and attacked the man, slamming his gun hand against the wall with his left. Dex moved his gun to shoot, but the guard grabbed his gun hand as well and grappled with Dex.

Dex lost his footing, and his back crashed against the stairs. He lost some strength in his grip, and his gun toppled. His enemy was on top of him and now had the advantage. Dex felt death approaching.

Reagan ran behind the guard, entangled her fingers in the back of the man's hair, and yanked hard. He yelped as his neck craned, and then Reagan smashed the side of his head against the metal railing twice. The sound reverberated like a baseball bat hitting a metal bar.

Reagan's action allowed Dex to climb to his feet, pick up his gun, and fire a shot through the underside of the man's chin. The bullet exited the top of his head along with a burst of blood, bone, and brains like an erupting volcano, and Dex threw the limp man over the railing.

Panting and sweating, he turned to Reagan then checked his kids. They were alive. He saw a strength in his wife he'd never seen before. *Oh, I love her,* he thought. He thanked her with a slight smile. She shrugged, and then they hurried to the landing and into the hall.

The echoes of a hundred stomping feet reached his ears. A group of ten men, led by Z, turned a corner and moved toward them. Dex glanced in the opposite direction and saw more men pouring in from a doorway.

Dex fired two quick shots toward Z and ushered his family back into the stairwell.

"Run! Up there!" Dex pointed, and they bolted.

He found a steel garbage can in the corner, moved it to the door, and angled it underneath the doorknob.

He tore up the stairs after his wife and kids and reached the next floor, and Reagan looked at him for direction. His gut told him to go to the top, so that was where he led them.

They stepped into an empty hall and caught their breath for a moment. Dex heard the men break through the blocked door two levels down and swarm the stairwell.

Dex led his family down the corridor, but there was no exit. There were two doors on either side of the wall, and that was it. His heart thumped.

Dex rushed to the first door and flung it open. The door led into an empty office. It sounded like the other men were almost at their level.

He crossed to the second door and opened it. Inside was a narrow stairway that led up. Another chance. He felt a sliver of hope. It bought a little more time, at least, and with any luck, it led to an exit. He took the stairs in seconds, and Dex burst through the door at the top, pointing his gun.

Dex didn't expect to see what he did. He lowered his weapon. "We're good." He turned to them and wiped the sweat from his brow.

Reagan and the kids stepped through the door while Dex hung back to protect them. The door at the bottom of the stairs opened, and Z popped in. Dex fired a shot, but Z moved at the same moment, and the bullet zipped past him.

Dex followed his family through and closed the door.

AUTHOR NOTES: *I love action and tension in stories, and things are about to get crazy. I took martial arts as a teenager, and I implemented a few of those moves in this story. For me, it's easier writing dialogue than action. Conversations come fluid to me, where the action scenes have to be carefully constructed and choreographed. It's important to me to keep action gritty and grounded.*

Chapter 10: The Abandoned Motel

Dex stepped down from the doorway into a tub. The tub was brown from filth, and a stained shower curtain hung on its last four hooks. Dex pushed through the plastic and guided his wife and children out of the tub. The small restroom consisted of a single sink and toilet, and light-blue tiles lined the walls. Dex felt like he'd stepped into something from the sixties. Reagan gave him an apprehensive look, and he shrugged.

"Where are we?" Noah asked.

"Well... we're in a bathroom," Reagan answered.

Dex opened the bathroom door, peeking with his gun aimed, then stepped out into a bedroom. The bed and furniture were covered in dust and debris, the mattress sagged, and he saw the window and door to the outside. They were inside a motel room. It was old and run-down and appeared to be deserted.

He quickly ushered his family to the front door and told them to wait. Then he jogged back to the bathroom, to the door above the tub, and listened for any sound. It was silent. It was as if the men chasing them had simply stopped at the bottom of the stairwell. It didn't make sense, but Dex's priority was to get his family to safety, so he trotted back to them.

Noah stepped to the front door and placed his hand on the knob to turn it, but Dex yelled, "Stop! Don't open that, Noah. Let Daddy do it." Noah nodded and backed away.

Dex peeled back the drapes, a cloud of dust escaped, and he looked through the film-covered window. The glass was so filthy that it was hard to get a good vision, but the outside appeared to be clear.

He cautiously opened the door and stepped outside. A brisk breeze hit him, rain clouds crept above, and the tiny light of the sunset peeked through.

The walkway was empty. The parking lot was vacant. The air tasted delicious.

Dex noticed that the door held the number 8. Guarded, Reagan stepped out and took in their surroundings. Dex smiled, but the grin wiped away fast as he put them in a race again.

"We have to keep moving. We're not in the clear just yet."

"Where are we?" Reagan asked.

"I don't know."

A car zoomed by on the road in front of the motel. They hurried to the street and looked in both directions. It was a highway. Dex didn't see any oncoming vehicles, but he saw a light in the distance. It was a gas station, maybe a mile or so away.

The four of them trekked toward it, huddling close, and Dex kept a wary eye out for danger. He turned his head to look back at the motel a hundred times at least, but no one followed. The darkened, gray motel stared back at him like a ghost town holding secrets. Dex could only imagine the nightmares it held.

The adrenalin and fear didn't leave his body and probably wouldn't for a long time. Perhaps he'd feel a shade of it for the rest of his life. The closer they got to the gas station and the farther away from the motel, the better he felt.

The sign on the side of the road came into view. It was a Flying J truck stop. The interior was empty except for the attendant. They entered the store in their bare feet and dirty and torn pajamas, and they had several bruises and cuts. They startled the young man out of a deep stupor of boredom. He turned to them with bugged-out eyes and an open mouth.

"Police," Dex stammered.

After a moment, the twenty-something attendant nodded and turned to make the call, but Reagan stopped him.

"Where are we?"

The worker scrunched his face as if he hadn't heard her right.

"What city?" Reagan demanded.

"Wichita. A few miles out," the young man said finally.

"Kansas?" Dex asked rhetorically.

"Uh, yeah."

DEX STOOD NEXT TO A patrol car, a gray blanket draped around his shoulders, and Reagan and the kids sat in the back seat. They wore the same type of blankets. The red and blue lights flashed silently against the night, and three other police cars, parked askew, sat nearby.

Sheriff Sam Hendershot approached Dex after speaking with his deputy. "There's a Holiday Inn just down the road. We can put your family up there for the night and let you get some rest, and tomorrow we'll finish this up. We have what we need for now."

Dex glanced at his wife and then back at Hendershot. "We can't stay in this town. Not for another minute."

"Mr. Sanders, I understand, but there'll be more questions to answer in the morning. I just can't bear to put you and your family through that right now. You've been through enough. I'm posting a patrol outside your hotel. We'll keep you safe. I promise."

Dex didn't want to stay in a hotel, but the thought of going back to their house, the scene of the crime, frightened him. "I don't have any money," Dex said. "Not on me, anyway. I don't have my wallet. So I can't—"

"Don't worry 'bout that. I know the owner, and he's cuttin' me a deal. There's a twenty-four-hour diner close by. I'll have Sergeant Neal get you whatever food you want and bring it to you at the hotel." Hendershot's words were comforting.

"And we don't need a hospital," Dex answered before Hendershot could suggest it. He assumed he would. "We'll be all right."

Hendershot didn't respond.

"And you'll check out the deserted motel? They're still there. A lot of men with guns," Dex said.

Hendershot's eyes shifted to the left, and he adjusted his belt. Dex saw doubt cross his eyes. "We will. We're waitin' on a team to arrive as we speak." Hendershot gave a courtesy smile.

"Thank you."

AUTHOR NOTES: *I've stayed in a lot of bad motels in my life. Not as bad as an abandoned one, but I remember ignoring a cockroach or two. Not my most pleasant of memories. I needed to put the compound for the bad guys in a hidden place. Somewhere least expected. I drove from Denver to Fort Smith, Arkansas, once, and while passing through the western part of Kansas, the land was flat and desolate, which made it perfect for this location. The idea just popped in my head, and I went with it.*

Chapter 11: Short Reprieve

Sergeant Neal was a sharp young man and was courteous to the Sanders family. He checked them into the hotel, led them to the room, and made sure they were comfortable. He gave them options for food. The kids resoundingly wanted pizza, and Neal's face broke into a wide grin, and he said, "I know just the place."

The pizza was good, and they devoured it like they'd never eaten before. Sergeant Neal brought several types of soda pop back as well as water bottles.

Neal and three other officers chatted outside their room while they ate and settled in. Reagan and Dex bathed the kids, put them in their bed, and found a SpongeBob cartoon for them to watch, and they were out in fifteen minutes.

Dex ran a bath and slowly lowered his body into the hot water. Each puncture wound from the needle chair sang at a high pitch, and he gritted his teeth. He washed his face with a cloth and lay back.

Reagan stepped into the bathroom and sat down on the toilet seat, looking at Dex. Her eyes wandered across his body, and tears filled them. Dex looked at the hundreds of red, pin-sized dots. She had to wonder what they were.

"Hi, sweetie." Dex managed a smile.

"Hi, babe. How're you feeling?" Reagan asked.

"Better now. We're alive and away from that place."

"I can't believe it. You saved us. I... I can't begin to process how you did it. You just took over. With so much confidence. It was like watching someone else. And how you..."

She didn't have to finish. Dex filled the blank in his mind. *Killed people.*

"How did you do it?"

"I didn't have a choice. They were going to kill you and the kids. I reacted on instinct."

"But you fought like Chuck Norris or something. Like you've done this before." She squinted.

"It was a first for me. Do you remember me telling you about my training when I was younger? About Jack Bennett?"

"He was your karate instructor, right? And he took you in when your parents died," she said.

"Yes. He trained me in martial arts, grappling, and weaponry. We ran millions of scenarios from hand-to-hand combat to how to disarm an enemy and the use of weapons. I learned how to read an enemy's body movements, speech, and all sorts of stuff. He was a marine, and he put me through a lot of the same training. However, I've never had to use it before, and it's been years since I did any of that. But it came back like riding a bike."

"It certainly paid off."

"Yes." He nodded emphatically. "And Jack Bennett's name came up several times in their questions. I think... No, I'm sure this has something to do with him. I don't know what he was into. He never told me anything."

"Is that why they came after us? Took us from our home?"

"No. That's the strange thing. Someone pointed a finger at us. Used us as a deterrent."

"Who?"

"Wes Chamberlain."

Reagan gasped. "Wes and Olive?"

"Yeah, can you believe it? That's why they haven't been home for so long."

Her face wrinkled with anger. "Those bastards! Why would they do that to us? To our family? We have kids, for hell's sake. So, they're involved with these assholes?"

"Yes. As I look back, I can see it. Wes always acted strangely. Like he was faking conversation, and he seemed very secretive too. They never let anyone in their house except us, and that was only if it was prescheduled."

"And they had those weird meetings in the middle of the night. A few months ago, remember? I saw a bunch of men come over to their house at one thirty in the morning. They met in their garage, and the light was on all night," Reagan said.

"I remember. You woke me up," Dex said, nodding.

"We've got to tell the police about them," Reagan groused. "We did nothing wrong. They targeted innocent people. I can't believe they did that. What I'd like to do to them." Heat rose in her face.

"We won't be seeing them again." Dex's voice was somber.

"How's that?"

"They're dead."

She sat back against the toilet as if hit by an invisible force.

"Those men put them through the same hell we just went through, only they didn't make it."

Reagan gulped.

Changing subjects, Dex asked, "Did you call your sister?"

She nodded. "Yes. She's going to stop by our house in the morning and pick up some clothes and things. I told her to have the police escort her there. Those men could still be there. Who knows?"

"Then she's driving out here to pick us up?"

"Yes. Probably around ten or eleven. I guess we'll go back to her place. I don't know."

"Sheriff Hendershot said we need to answer more questions in the morning." Dex started scrubbing his body with soap. "Possibly means a trip to the station and signing a statement. I'll let you and the kids go with Pam, and I'll stay back to answer their questions."

"No," she blurted. "We are not separating. Not again."

"I just didn't want you guys to have to hang around. It could take hours."

"It doesn't matter. I'll make Hendershot get that shit done fast." She pursed her lips.

Dex chuckled.

Reagan looked at his wounds again. "How *are* you? What are all these tiny holes? What did they do to you?"

Dex told her everything from the beginning, as softly as he could, continuing to reassure her that he was going to be okay. Dex finished his bath and convinced Reagan she'd feel better if she took one too. She fought it at first, just wanting to curl up in bed with him, but she finally surrendered and took her bath.

While she was bathing, a knock came at the door, and hairs perked up on the back of Dex's neck. He wished he still had his gun. The police had confiscated it, and he was weaponless. If the bad men showed up again, he'd lost his element of surprise, and they'd have the advantage.

Peeking through the drapes, he saw Hendershot at the door. He half smiled and waved at Dex through the window. Dex opened the door and stepped outside.

Hendershot stood straight with his back arched, beer gut popping forward, and a toothpick cockily stuck in his mouth.

"Sanders." He nodded with a sly grin.

"Sheriff. Tell me you found something."

"Wish I could." He shook his head. "I gotta tell ya, this is one of the most cockamamie stories I've ever heard. In all my twenty-five years on the force, I've never heard such a thing. The more a story doesn't make sense, the less truth there is in it. And this... something's afoot, and I'm going to get to the bottom of it."

He gave Dex an accusing look that crawled under his skin.

"What are you talking about?" Dex demanded. "You went to room 8, right? Into the bathroom? The strange door inside?"

"Oh yeah, and we found the door all right. It was locked, and we busted the thing open. Nothing but a brick wall behind it. So against my better judgment, I gave you the benefit of the doubt and busted through that wall. There weren't nothin.'"

"That can't be. We came out of there. How can you explain everything? Our abduction from our home, our wounds, and our trauma?"

"A lot of crazy shit happens in this world. I don't like it, but many times, it's up to me to wade through that shit and figure it all out. And most of the time, I find the answer staring me square in the face."

"I don't understand." Dex narrowed his eyes.

"Did you two have an argument? Trouble on the home front?"

Flabbergasted, Dex said, "Oh, come on."

He held his hands up. "Hey, look. I get it. Maybe you're going through a lot of depression, hard times, maybe lost your job, maybe you lost your girlfriend. Hell, maybe she caught you and your girlfriend, and you lost your mind. Decided it was the end of you two and that you were taking your kids with you." He stabbed a finger at him. "I've seen it a million times, and it disgusts me to the bone, Mr. Sanders." He looked at his wounds. "Looks to me like she fought back. Won too. There's a lot of investigation yet to go, and I'll get to the bottom of this. I guaran-damn-tee you."

Dex glared.

"Honestly, I hope you're right, Sanders. I do. But if you're not, there'll be hell to pay."

"No, Sheriff," Dex said. "You'd better hope I'm not right."

AUTHOR NOTES: *The Sanderses were safe for a moment, and they got a night to heal their wounds and get some needed rest. I have a wife and two boys of my own, and the Sanders family continues to remind me*

of them. Of course, I inject a lot of my own experiences into these characters to give them life, and then I ask myself, what would I do in this situation?

Chapter 12: The Chase

Dex chose not to tell Reagan about his conversation with Sheriff Hendershot. At least not for the moment.

As tired as he was, Dex didn't get much sleep. Every hour, he woke up and found himself peering out the window. The patrol car was in the parking lot below them, and each time he looked, he saw the officer sitting inside. His head was tilted forward slightly, like he was looking at his phone. He'd wait until he saw some activity. A movement of the cop's arm or a twisting of his head, just enough to convince Dex that the officer was still awake and *alive*.

Dex finally found some sleep in the last two hours of the morning. He slept straight through until 7:45. He heard his boys whispering to each other and shuffling in the covers. He smiled. It was good to see them alive, talking, moving, and giggling. Nothing warmed his heart more. He'd been so close to death. They had been too. He'd nearly lost them, and now he wanted to cherish every minute he had with them.

As thankful as Dex was, he was equally terrified of losing them. Whatever mess this was, it was far from being over. Yes, they'd escaped but not without damage. He'd killed at least four men and ratted them out to the police. There'd be retribution.

Reagan woke up and popped out of bed. She glanced at her phone. "We have to get going. Pam will be here in ten minutes."

Dex helped Reagan wrangle the kids into the bathroom to get them dressed and ready.

When a knock came at the door, Dex and Reagan shared startled looks. It reminded Dex of how much they were both on edge.

"It's probably Pam," Reagan said.

He glanced through the drapes, staying away from the door in case the perpetrator chose to shoot through it. He saw Pam dressed in jeans, boots, a burgundy silk shirt, and a fashionable scarf. Two suitcases stood at her side.

He let out a sigh of relief and opened the door. The look on her face was a mix of tension, confusion, and grief.

"*Dex.* Oh my gosh, are you okay? I can't *believe.*"

They hugged, and Reagan and the boys quickly ran to embrace her as well.

"I hope I brought enough. I grabbed clothes for the boys, undies and socks, and their toothbrushes and things. I didn't know what you two liked." She gestured to Dex and Reagan. "Neither of you had much in your closet or dressers. I need to take you shopping." She shifted her eyes to her sister, and Reagan chuckled.

"Did you grab my makeup case and curling iron?" Reagan asked.

"Yes, I brought your lifeboat."

"Oh, thank you." Reagan sighed.

"How was the house?" Dex asked. "Did the police escort you?"

"Yes. Two fine officers. One of them exceptionally tall, handsome, and built like Conan the Barbarian." She fluttered her eyelashes with admiration. "The house was okay. It was in a bit of a mess but, other than that, nothing weird."

"Well, I'm glad you're safe," Reagan said.

"We'd better hurry," Dex said and walked to the window. He looked out at the patrol car. It was still parked in the same spot, and he saw the cop still sitting upright inside.

"Reagan, I'll get the kids ready. You go ahead and finish yourself, okay?" Pam said.

"Thanks." She ran to the sink and plugged in her curling iron.

They were ready in a record twenty minutes, and Dex checked on the cop car outside again. Nothing had changed. The cop hadn't moved, and Dex felt a tingle of suspicion.

"We're ready to go," Reagan said to Dex. "Is everything okay?"

"Yeah," he said hesitantly. "It's just... I haven't heard from the police or Hendershot. I thought I'd get a call by now or someone would come to our door."

"Let's get something to eat first. We're hungry, and we can call him on the road."

Dex stepped out first and cautiously led them down the walkway to the stairs and then crossed the parking lot to Pam's shiny black Lexus GX SUV.

He kept his eyes on the police car as his family filed into the SUV.

"Give me a minute," Dex said to Reagan and Pam before striding over to the squad car.

As he approached the half-open window of the driver's side, he heard buzzing and saw flies, and his gut sank. Sergeant Neal's throat was split open. It looked like a jagged clown smile below his real mouth. Blood drenched his front. His face had turned gray, and his body was slumped forward so his chin rested on his chest. Duct tape strapped his upper body to the seat, and tape was also wrapped underneath his chin and the headrest as if to hold him upright and appear to be alive, but the tape had loosened, causing his head to tilt forward. By the look of the coagulated blood, it appeared that he'd been dead for a while.

Dex stepped back and quickly scanned the area but saw nothing out of the ordinary.

Pam started the engine and began to drive the SUV toward Dex to pick him up, when Dex signaled to her with his hands for her to stop. He trotted to her window.

"Everything okay?" Reagan poked her head out the back window.

He nodded with a grave look in his eyes.

"Fine, fine. Sure. Uh, Pam, can I use your phone?"

"Yeah." She reached into her purse and handed it to him.

"I'm just going to call Sheriff Hendershot first, okay?"

Reagan didn't argue.

Dex stepped away from the vehicle, withdrew Hendershot's business card from his pocket, and called him. A man picked up after two rings.

"Hello?"

Dex expected Hendershot to answer with his title and name or at least "Sheriff's Office. How can I help you?' He didn't get any of that.

"Sheriff Hendershot?" Dex asked.

"Mr. Sanders. You know, I miss you already." Dex recognized that smooth voice with an undercurrent of smugness. It was all he'd heard for the past couple of days. "Did you have an emergency?" Dr. H asked.

"*Bastard.*"

"You started this little game, Mr. Sanders. I'm going to finish it."

The call disconnected. Panic set in, and his mind spun.

Where is Hendershot? Where are the police? Are they all dead? And how am I and my family still alive?

"Pam, do you mind if I drive?" Dex jogged back to the Lexus.

She slid out of the seat with no question. She took Reagan's spot in the back, and Reagan took the passenger's side up front.

"Did you get ahold of Hendershot?" Reagan asked, her eyebrows raised.

"Sort of." He looked at the reflection of his kids in the rearview. Their wide eyes were locked on him. "Hey, Aunt Pam's got a new game on her phone you guys can play."

Pam scrunched her face. "I do?"

"I'm sure you do. Or a movie, something to keep the kids occupied, perhaps?"

"Oh, yeah." She finally took the hint to distract the boys.

"Do you have Soda Crush?" Jacob asked.

"Of course."

Dex stretched his right hand over to Reagan, grasped hers, and whispered, "He didn't make it."

"Hendershot?"

"No. Sergeant Neal. In the police car."

Her face drained of all color, and she gulped.

"I called Hendershot, and the man from... you know... there? The one they call Dr. H. He answered."

She gripped his hand like a vise.

"This isn't over?" Her question came out like a whimper.

He held her eyes with his. "We're going to get through this."

They stopped at a McDonald's near the freeway, picked up food from the drive-through, and drove onto I-75 toward their home in Denver.

An hour into the drive, Dex noticed a blue Toyota Corolla behind them. Two men sat in the front, but he couldn't make out their faces. They'd been behind them for twenty minutes.

Dex slowed down and merged into the far-right lane. The car followed him. He let up on the gas, letting the speed fall to fifty-five. He drove that speed for the next few minutes, and the car stayed with him. Everyone behind the Toyota moved to the next lane and passed them.

"Why are you going so slowly?" Reagan asked.

"See that blue car back there?" He kept his voice low, and Reagan nodded after casting a quick glance over her shoulder. "They've been following us for a while. I dropped my speed so low anyone in their right mind would pass us, but he's not."

"I can't do this." Panic rose in Reagan's voice. "We need to call the police."

"We can't," he snapped. "They've been compromised. One of their own was killed, and that psycho answered Sheriff Hendershot's phone. Going to them now could be sealing our fate. I don't know who to trust."

"What the hell do you suggest, Dex? We can't keep doing this."

"I know. I know. We need to go to a safe place."

"We could go to my condo," Pam suggested from the back seat.

Dex shook his head. "No, I don't want to lead anybody there. We need to go to my brother's."

"Conner?" Reagan questioned him.

Conner was Dex's brother from another mother... and father. Like Dex, Conner was an orphan whom Jack Bennett had taken in. Dex and Conner trained together and became as close as brothers could be. Conner took a different path from Dex, leading him into a violent life of underground mixed martial arts fighting. It involved gambling and drugs and put him in jail a couple of times.

"He can help protect us," Dex said.

"He may be the one who got us into this mess. Because of the people he deals with," Reagan grumbled.

"You know who got us into this," Dex said, referring to their neighbor, Wes.

Reagan nodded. "I know. It's just... I worry about Conner."

"He has weapons and connections that may help us. I'm sure he has an arsenal."

Dex took Interstate 25 toward the city and yanked the car to the right at the last minute onto an exit. To Dex's surprise, the Corolla missed the exit and continued south on 25.

"I think we lost them," Reagan said.

But Dex shrugged uneasily. He wasn't so sure. He headed west and, two blocks down, caught sight of a silver Ford Focus behind them. Through his rearview, he saw the silhouettes of two men inside.

"Either I'm paranoid, or we have more company."

Reagan craned her head, and her eyes widened.

"They're everywhere," she whispered in a shaky voice.

Dex drove along a busy street through two lights and stopped at a red light. He was the first on the line, and the Focus was right behind him. He looked left and right at the cars on the opposite street as their light turned green. At the very moment cars inched into the intersection, Dex pressed the gas pedal and shot the Lexus forward. He passed through the crossroads as a pickup truck halted, tires squealing, and came within inches of hitting their vehicle. The air rang with an assortment of honks, and Dex heard a man curse at him through an open window.

Dex's heart pounded, and he saw Reagan white-knuckle-gripping the armrest. He glanced in the rearview mirror and saw that the Focus had attempted the same trick and nearly caused an accident. The Focus was now trapped by oncoming traffic.

Dex glanced at the back seat and saw the shocked look on Pam's and Jacob's faces. Jacob appeared more confused, while Noah was oblivious. He was too involved with the game in his hands.

"Made it. We're fine." Dex forced a smile, attempting to shake away the nerves from his jittering body.

AUTHOR NOTES: *A number of years ago, I worked in Denver for a period of time, so I thought this city would be perfect for Dex and his family to live in. When I left Denver to go to my next work location, I drove through the emptiness of Kansas, which turned out to be a perfect spot for the abandoned motel and the underground compound. Now the Sanderses are on the run. I've lit the fuse, and it won't stop until the explosive ending.*

Chapter 13: Brother from Another Mother

The tires of the Lexus crunched loose gravel as Dex drove up to the single-wide trailer and parked. The mobile home was beaten down and rusted and stood on a slant. It sat among trees and brush in the middle of nowhere.

Dex noticed hesitation in the eyes of his wife and Pam, and a slight doubt grew in the back of his head too.

He exited the vehicle and approached the front door and knocked. His family hung back. It took a few more knocks and almost two minutes before muted sounds were heard from within, and the door finally opened. He turned his head at the horrid stench of stale smoke and alcohol that hit him.

Conner stood in the doorway, half-open eyes, scarecrow hair, and nothing on but an old robe and boxers. He scratched his hairy chest through the opening and yawned.

"Dex? What the hell?" Conner grumbled.

"We need your help," Dex said.

Conner ran his eyes over the bruises on his face and marks on his bare arms, and his jaw dropped. "Shit yeah, ya do. Come in. Come in." Conner glanced at the family behind him and smiled sheepishly. "Place is a wreck. You'll have to forgive, but mi casa, su casa."

Conner held the door as they all ambled in, and Pam's eyes darted to his boxers where his drawbridge gaped open, and she gasped. Conner quickly closed it and gave her a wink and a greasy smile.

Conner jogged to the sofa and pushed piles of junk and clothes off it. "Here. Take a seat. Boys, you like Xbox?"

Conner quickly got Jacob and Noah set up to play games, and Reagan sat behind them on the couch. Pam rested her butt on the edge, and Conner and Dex stepped into the kitchen for a private talk.

"Beer?" Conner asked as he opened the fridge and pulled out a bottle.

"This early?" Dex questioned him.

"It's the best thing for a hangover, and I got a bad one."

He popped off the cap and took a swig, and they sat across from each other at his small table. Conner shifted his eyes in the direction of the front room, where the family was, and said, "This has got to be killing Reagan to be here."

"She's fine," Dex said.

"You sure about that?"

"Conner, we need your help. We have no place to go."

Conner lowered his eyes to the beer in his hand and said in a low voice, "I know how that is."

"I'm sorry about what happened last year," Dex said. Conner had been released on parole and had nowhere to go. He'd asked Dex if he could stay with them for a couple of weeks until he found a place. "I wanted to let you stay..."

"Hey. You don't have to make excuses. Reagan was right. It wouldn't have been good if I'd moved in. I'm not exactly a good role model for the kids to be around."

"It may not seem like it, but Reagan does like you."

Conner raised his eyebrows.

"Really. She does." Dex nodded. "She's just too stubborn to show it."

"So, what kind of trouble are you in?" Conner shifted topics. "You look like you've been run over by a truck."

"I feel like it." Dex sighed, and it took nearly twenty-five minutes to fill him in on what had happened.

Conner had finished his second beer and pulled a third from the fridge. "You sure you don't want one?" he offered Dex again.

Dex shook his head.

Conner sat back down and cracked it open. "So, what's the plan?"

Dex shrugged. "I'm not sure. I want to go to the police, but I've already done that, and it nearly cost us our lives. I'm not sure we can trust them right now."

"Cops just muddy up the water, Dex. I have a friend you should go see. He's a private dick. A real good one, and he's gotten me out of a tight spot or two. I trust him more than I trust myself. We'll set him loose like a bloodhound to track those men down and find out who they are. Once we know who we're dealing with, we can make a plan. He'll know what to do."

CONNER SLIPPED A 9MM semiautomatic pistol into the palm of Dex's hand along with an extra clip. "For protection."

"Thanks."

Conner turned to Reagan, who stood next to Dex at the front door. Her face was clenched tight, and her eyes shifted nervously.

"This one's for you." Conner handed her a smaller pistol. "Not as much kick. Figured you could handle it. Do you know how to use it?"

"Point and shoot, right?" she asked.

"Right." Conner grinned. "Just remember the safety is right here." He pointed at it on the gun.

She rolled her eyes. "I know. I'm not stupid."

"I know you're not."

She exhaled, and some tension released from her shoulders. "Conner..." She struggled to find words.

"I know," Conner said as if reading her thoughts. "And look…" He placed a hand over his heart. "I got your boys. With my *life*. I promise."

Tears welled, and she gave him a nod. "I know you do." She hugged him as if to seal the deal and then turned to Pam and her boys, who were still in front of the TV. "You boys be good, okay?" she called to them. "Listen to everything Pam and Conner tell you."

"We will," Jacob called without turning from his game.

Noah gave a grunt.

"I got 'em," Pam reassured her. "You two be safe."

"We will. Love you," Reagan said to all of them, and she exited with Dex.

Once the door was closed, Conner sauntered to the couch and sat next to Pam. He wore a large grin. "I guess it's just us."

She spread a fake smile and looked away.

"Want a beer?" Conner asked.

"You got a Starbucks Frappuccino with extra pumps of frap?"

He shook his head. "I do have coffee and a pumpkin spice creamer."

"No shit?"

DEX PULLED INTO A PARKING space in front of a three-story brown apartment building, and he and Reagan exited the car. As they walked to the entrance, Reagan touched his arm, and he turned to her.

"Are we doing the right thing? Do we even know this guy?" she asked.

"I trust Conner. He wouldn't steer us wrong."

She took in a deep, rattled breath.

"Hey. You trust me, right?"

"With everything."

"I won't let anything happen. To you or the kids."

She nodded, and he kissed her on the forehead. They continued to the stairwell, climbed to the second floor, and knocked on the door that read 2B. The door frame was cracked, and a chunk of wood was missing. Dex also noticed a dent next to the handle. *Looks like he's had some trouble,* he thought.

Geoff Hanover was a large, burly man with a gruff voice and a full beard. He reminded Dex of the animated character Yukon Cornelius from *Rudolph the Red-Nosed Reindeer*. He had all the features of sandpaper, yet his eyes were gentle.

"You must be Conner's brother, Dex," he said and turned to Reagan with an upturned smile. "And his lovely wife, Mrs. Sanders."

"You can call me Reagan." She returned the smile.

Dex looked at Geoff's right arm, which was bandaged up to the elbow. The center of it was red. As if feeling Dex's gaze, Geoff placed his left hand over it.

"Well, come on in. It's not much, but make yourself at home. Any friend of Conner's and all that."

Dex and Reagan entered and sat down on his sofa. Dex was not surprised to see the apartment filled with outdoor décor. His fireplace mantel was a log that looked like it was cut out of a tree, lacquered, and nailed to the wall. Geoff had a coat rack made of antlers, and a large stuffed bass hung above the couch along with paintings of bears and one of a man fly-fishing in a river. He was already impressed by the immaculate cleanliness that was opposite of Conner's.

"Can I get ya anything? A beer maybe or some water?" Geoff offered.

"I could use some water," Reagan answered.

"Comin' right up." Geoff entered the kitchen and talked to them as he took a glass out of the cupboard. "Conner said you're in a bit of a pickle."

"You could say that," Dex replied, sighing heavily.

"He gave me the shortened version on the phone. Pretty wild." Geoff walked back to them. He placed a glass of water in Reagan's hand then sat down in a chair opposite them. "And the authorities won't help?"

"They tried to at first," Dex said. "In Wichita, but they didn't believe us. Then the cop they posted to protect us wound up dead."

"And that makes you think the cops are involved?" Geoff scrunched his eyes.

"Not exactly, but when I called Sheriff Hendershot, our captor answered instead. And that's not the only thing. I found it odd that when the police arrived, they didn't call an ambulance or take us to the hospital. I thought it would be protocol after what we'd been through."

"Especially for Dex," Reagan pointed out. "I mean, look at him."

Geoff nodded and said, "Yes, you look like you've been cage fighting with Conner." He chuckled. "Okay, so cops are out of the question for now. At some point, we'll have to involve them, and when we do, I have some trusted friends on the force we can go to. But first let's find out who we're dealing with and why they seem to be after you."

Geoff's words came out with confidence. Dex liked hearing that Geoff had trusted friends on the force. Suddenly he felt they'd made the right choice, coming to Geoff. Dex looked at Reagan and saw the same relief in her expression.

Geoff locked his eyes with Dex's as if searching. "You don't know why these guys might be after you?"

"No. Unless I sold them a bad car." He chuckled with no humor.

"Anyone at work acting suspicious lately? Friends, relatives, anyone?" Geoff looked at each of them.

"Just our neighbors. Wes and Olive Chamberlain. We're in this mess because of them."

"They gave our names to the bad guys and told them *we're* the ones they're looking for," Reagan added with anger heightening in her voice.

"And they tortured and questioned you?" Geoff gestured to Dex.

"Yes."

"What questions did they ask?"

Dex widened his eyes and exhaled. "They started with my childhood. They talked about my parents' deaths and how I was raised by my karate instructor, Jack Bennett. I'm pretty sure it has something to do with him. They wouldn't let it go."

"Where is Jack Bennett now?"

"I have no clue. He disappeared from my life years ago."

"Hmm." Geoff looked away as if processing what he'd heard. "There's got to be something else. What exactly did they want from you?"

"They think I'm part of some group they're in direct conflict with. Like a rebel army of some sort. They wanted to know where their base was," Dex said with a hint of incredulousness.

"And you don't have any idea of who this army is or any connection it has to you?"

"No."

"The connection is with Wes and Olive. Clearly, they're the ones they're after, and they pointed a finger at us to throw them off the real trail," Reagan said.

Geoff nodded and leaned back. "What was Wes and Olive's behavior like leading up to this? Did they do anything odd? When's the last time you interacted with them?"

Reagan shook her head, trying to think. "I don't know. Probably a month ago, I guess. I talked to Olive while I was doing some yard work. I asked her about how her husband's work was going and things like that. She asked the same about us but nothing unusual."

"Wait." An idea popped into Dex's head. "When I got home the other night, there was a strange package sent to me in the mail. It didn't have a return address, and I don't think it had any postage either, which means someone other than a mailman put it in our box."

"What was inside?" Geoff asked.

"I don't know. I didn't open it. I didn't think much of it."

"It could be something." Geoff rubbed his bandaged arm, and Dex noticed the blood circle had widened.

"Are you *okay*? What happened?" Dex asked.

"Oh this?" Geoff pointed at his wound, sounding surprised. "It's nothing. Cut myself while I was dicing vegetables earlier. I'm not much of a chef." He chuckled. Geoff shifted his eyes once to Reagan and then back to Dex. "I'll do some background research on your neighbors. I'll make a call and get someone on that. As for you..." He pointed at Dex. "We need to go to your house and retrieve that package. Let's find out what's in it. It could be something. Could be nothing."

AUTHOR NOTES: *Conner is a fun character who, in many ways, is the opposite of Dex. He also happens to be a badass dude. Both Conner and Reagan's sister, Pam, help balance the story. We're also about to embark on some cool action. A fan of mine compared my writing, particularly my Damage Inc. novels, to Don Pendleton's. A huge compliment. I read many of his Executioner series of action books as a teen, so I'm not surprised if some of his styles sneak into my books.*

Chapter 14: Followed

Following Geoff's pickup truck, Dex kept wary of suspicious cars, but so far, he hadn't noticed anyone trailing them. He looked ahead and focused on Geoff's head through the back window of the old Ford. Dex's eyes narrowed as he questioned Geoff's loyalty. *Can we really trust him?* Something seemed off here. He shifted his eyes to Reagan, whose fingers were busy texting Pam.

"Are Pam and the boys okay?"

"Yeah." She sighed. "They're still playing video games. Conner fed them some snacks. Fish crackers and granola bars."

"That's a relief." Dex returned his eyes to the road.

Reagan rubbed Dex's shoulder. It felt like a boulder.

"You're really tense."

Dex nodded. "I hope there's no surprises at our house. What if they're waiting for us? What if—" Dex was too afraid to say it out loud.

"What if what?" Reagan pressed.

"I get a funny feeling about Geoff," Dex said.

"What do you mean? You said he was Conner's friend, so you trust him."

"I do, but... something's not right. Did you see that bandage around his arm?"

"Yes."

"Blood was seeping through it. It's bad. He said it happened while he was dicing vegetables. How did he slice his forearm while cutting up veggies? Fingers, yes, but your *forearm*?"

Reagan nodded. "True. But it could happen, I suppose."

"Very unlikely," Dex mumbled.

"I was the unsure one at first, but after talking with him, he seems very genuine. Trustworthy."

"I know. I was, too, until he told me what happened to his arm. I just want us to be cautious. As a matter of fact, we can't trust anyone other than Conner and your sister. It's not safe."

"Are you saying we shouldn't follow Geoff?"

"No. We will. For now. Let's just be careful. Trust only goes so far."

DEX PARKED BEHIND GEOFF in front of their house. No other vehicles were there. Dex stared at his home for a moment in silence. It was a surreal feeling, looking at his house for the first time since the incident. It was marked with the trauma and fear from that night. It held a past he wanted to forget.

"No one was here when Pam came," Reagan said.

"You're right. Let's go."

They exited the vehicle, and Geoff and Dex withdrew their pistols. Geoff carried a silver .357 Magnum.

"You got some stopping power," Dex remarked, and Geoff gave him a devilish look. Dex turned to Reagan. "You have your gun?"

"It's in my purse." She patted the side of it. "I think you two have us covered."

Geoff entered the house first, pointing his gun, and cleared the first floor quickly. He motioned for Dex and Reagan to follow. They stepped in and began to inspect their home. A hand flew to Reagan's mouth as she gasped.

The living room sofa was torn apart. Its stuffing bulged through the shredded leather. The love seat and La-Z-Boy were the same, the TV was smashed in and lying on the floor, and papers and knickknacks covered the house like the aftermath of a tornado.

It was a sick feeling for Dex to see all their furniture and possessions torn apart. It gave him the sensation that all was lost. With their current financial struggles, it would be difficult to replace it all.

Dex slid the metal chamber back on his 9mm, engaging the first bullet, and entered the kitchen while Geoff travelled upstairs.

All their cabinets were open, and one of them was dangling on one hinge. All their drawers had been pulled out and tossed to the ground. Glasses and dishes were strewn about, many broken. Dex's shoes crunched over glass. He began moving items around on the counter, looking for the package, but couldn't find it.

"Do you remember what you did with it?" Reagan asked.

"This is where we usually leave the mail." He looked at the counter, perplexed. "Wait. I took it upstairs with me. Remember? I tried to open it, but I needed a knife."

Dex stepped to where the utensil drawer was, but the drawer was pulled out and sat upside down on top of a mix of utensils. He rummaged through, found a knife, and approached the stairs.

"Upstairs is clear!" Geoff called down to them.

Dex cautiously ascended with his gun at the ready. He wasn't taking any chances with Geoff. For all he knew, he could be waiting to shoot them.

He was not. The hall was clear, and Dex entered his bedroom with Reagan.

His stomach sank when he saw their bed torn apart and clothes thrown everywhere.

"Bastards," Reagan said.

The lamp from his nightstand was thrown down, and nothing sat on top of it. He quickly searched and then pulled the nightstand from the wall. Wedged between the nightstand and the wall was the box. He grabbed it, sat down, and stabbed the knife through the tape.

"It's probably nothing. What if it's a promotional offer like we thought?"

"Then it is." Reagan lifted her hands as if to say, *Oh well.*

Geoff poked his head through the doorway.

"It's a book." Dex withdrew a paperback from inside. It was titled *The Mind's Eye*, by Jon Radcliff. The cover was black except for an image of a brain with an eye situated in the center of it. "It looks like science fiction."

"Anything inside it?" Geoff asked.

Dex flipped through it and stopped at the second page in.

"Whoever sent it wrote something here. It says, *Read this. Keep your mind open. There is so much to learn here. It's extremely important. – W.C.*

"Wes Chamberlain?" Reagan asked.

"Anything else in there?" Geoff persisted.

"No," Dex said after flipping through the entire book. "It's just a normal book. He didn't write anything else."

"There may be some clues in it. Keep it and read it. You may find out more about Wes."

The screech of tires coming to a halt perked their senses.

Geoff's eyes widened. "I think we have company."

CONNER WATCHED PAM take a sip from her coffee mug. She hadn't moved from the edge of the couch since Dex and Reagan left. Although she wore a brave face, it was clear she wanted to jump out of her skin. He wished he could offer her a nicer couch to sit on or a better place to stay. She was attractive and dressed nicer than her situation merited.

Conner picked up a bottle and took a gulp. He'd replaced his beer with water. He needed to stay sober. He'd been tasked with watching Dex and Reagan's kids, and he wasn't about to mess that up. He was also cognizant of the danger that threatened them, and he didn't take it lightly. Conner turned his attention back to the video game the kids were playing.

"I've had this game for a year, and I never reached this level." Conner pointed at the screen, and Jacob giggled.

"I gave up competing with these kids a long time ago," Pam said and flashed him a smile. "You should try helping them with their homework."

It may have been her smile or the glint in her eyes, but something about her drew Conner in.

"You play these games with them?" Conner asked.

"I used to, but my pride can only take so much."

He kept his gaze on her as she watched the boys play. Her auburn hair, highlighted with blond, curved down the side of her face and slightly down her back. Her eyes were a dark chocolate, and her lips were full.

"What kind of conditioner do you use?" Conner asked suddenly.

She turned to him with a wrinkled brow and stuttered, "W-Wha—my conditioner?"

"Whatever it is, it makes your hair really shine."

She blushed and looked away then turned back to him. "I always use Paul Mitchell."

He nodded with a smile.

The sound of gravel crunching under tires made chills run up his spine.

"Is that the pizza?" Pam asked. Conner had called ten minutes ago and ordered food for all of them.

"If it is, they're in record time. Be ready to move, just in case," he warned her and cautiously moved to the entrance. Earlier he'd placed a .30-30 rifle next to the door. He picked it up as he peeked through the blinds.

A black SUV was parked out front, and a man approached his house, carrying an automatic rifle. Conner slowly opened the window a crack, cocked his rifle, and aimed it. The man was lined up in his sights, but Conner hesitated on pulling the trigger. If it was the FBI or some branch of the police, he didn't want to make the mistake of shooting at them. A sparkle flashed in the trees beyond and caught Conner's attention. *Sniper.*

He turned and yelled, "Pam! Get the kids and get down!"

Pam dived for the boys, tackling them, and they rolled just as a bullet penetrated the window and busted the TV.

Conner poked his rifle out the window, but the man walking toward his home was gone. He swiveled and fired two shots in the direction of the flash in the trees, and rapid gunfire erupted. A barrage of bullets peppered his trailer. Rounds busted holes in walls, blew apart cabinets, and smashed dishes, and some ricocheted.

Conner dropped to the floor until the firing stopped.

"Pam? You and the boys okay?" Conner asked.

"Y-Yes. What do we do now?"

Conner raised his head to the window and saw two men with guns, one running to the north of his house and the other to the south. He quickly took aim and shot, catching the second man in the hip.

The man yelped as his leg collapsed, and he went down. Conner shot again into the side of his head, and then the sniper fired. The bullet ripped through the side of Conner's arm below the shoulder.

Conner grunted and plopped back to the floor.

AUTHOR NOTES: *When I write, I picture everything playing out in my head like a movie. There were a few years where all I wrote were screenplays, which are a different beast altogether. When writing a screenplay, you have to convey everything you want in a very short amount of time. When I switched back to my original love of writing novels, I blended the two, and now my writing is quicker to the point. I don't like to waste a lot of time. If the pace slows down, it's because the characters or story calls for*

it. This next chapter is intense and nonstop, and would make a great action flick.

Chapter 15: Fight for Life

Geoff trotted down the hall and into the kids' room, where the window imploded and a man in dark fatigues flew in and tackled him. Geoff's back slammed to the floor, and his gun slipped out of his grip.

Dex moved to help Geoff then glimpsed three men at the bottom of the stairs in his peripheral vision. Automatic fire ripped up the walls of the stairway as Dex dove back into his room, tackling Reagan to the ground.

"You okay?" he asked her, and she nodded. "Do you have your gun? I have an idea."

She pulled the .22 pistol from her purse and handed it to Dex. Now he held a gun in each hand, waited at the doorway, and listened. He stuck his right hand into the open and quickly pulled it back as gunfire erupted.

Once the shooting stopped, Dex turned the corner and ran down the stairs, firing both guns. The men were halfway up the steps when Dex's bullets pounded into the two men in front. Blood spotted the walls, and the two men rocked back from the gunfire and toppled into the third man. Dex's momentum was too much for him to control, and he found himself amid the rolling ball of men.

Dex was quick to his feet once he hit the bottom floor, but the third man, unscathed by bullets, was faster. He snapped a front kick into Dex's chest, propelling him backward and over an end table. The guns flew from his hands as he hit the ground. He rolled and jumped to his feet in time to evade the swing of a knife at his throat. He blocked the attacker's knife arm, twisting the man around, and Dex pounded an uppercut to his left kidney.

The man groaned from the pain but slashed at Dex again. Dex was quick to block the blow with his right forearm and shot back a kick to the man's gut. He followed up with a left hook across his cheek and a powerful right punch to the man's face. Dex felt cartilage burst as the attacker's nose collapsed beneath his knuckles. Blood flew from the man's nostrils as he flew back against the wall.

Dex ran to the man and grabbed his throat in one hand and held the wrist of the attacker's knife hand in the other. As they both struggled, Dex saw a flash of silver in the man's eyes. It caught him off guard for just a second, but it was enough.

The man dug a knee into his groin, making Dex crumple in half. The attacker held the knife high above his head, preparing to stab it into Dex, when three pops stilled him. His eyes froze, and blood ran from his lips as he tripped and fell. Reagan stood a few feet away, holding her .22 pistol. Dex sighed with relief.

They both quickly ran to their kids' room to help Geoff, who was entangled with another man. The man was almost a whole head taller than Geoff, and he had him in a bear hug from behind. Geoff twisted and fought against his grasp. He looked at the wall in front of him and planted both feet against it. He then pushed off, shoving them both backward and through the broken window.

His opponent's back slammed against the roof overhang, and the full weight of Geoff's body smashed against his chest, releasing the man's hold on him. Geoff somersaulted over but grabbed the man and pulled him with him. Geoff scraped his right foot against the roof until it skidded to a stop against the gutter, but his enemy still slid toward him.

Geoff twisted, and with his hand still entangled in the man's jacket, he used his enemy's momentum to fling the man's body over the edge.

The man flew and landed with a loud crack on the windshield of the SUV parked in the driveway.

Geoff jumped the short distance to the ground, crouched, withdrew an extra pistol stowed in the back of his pants, and fired several shots into him. The driver's door popped open, and Geoff didn't skip a beat before turning and firing rounds. The bullets slammed through the SUV's door and window and opened the man's chest. Two rounds shot through the enemy's throat too. He gurgled, dropped to his knees, and toppled.

CONNER USHERED PAM and the kids down the hall past the kitchen then bent down and threw back a rug to reveal a latch in the floor. He lifted the door to reveal an open square filled with cobwebs.

"It leads to the ground beneath the trailer." He looked at both Pam and the boys. "You'll have to crawl, but we can make our way west into the cover of the trees."

"We can do it," Noah said bravely.

"W-What if they're waiting for us down there?" Pam stammered.

"They won't be," he reassured her. "I'll make sure of it. Here." He handed her a 9mm pistol. "Do you know how to fire it?"

"I think so," she said.

"Don't hesitate. Don't think. Just point and shoot."

He helped Pam down through the hatch and then lifted the boys down.

"Aren't you coming?" Pam looked up at him.

"I'll catch up. Go!"

He let the hatch door slam shut just as his front door flew open and a man ran in, shooting. Conner crouched and fired his rifle, cocked, refired, cocked, and fired again in rapid succession. The bullets hammered the man's chest, tearing open three red holes.

Two more, Conner thought as he crawled toward the dead body. *The first man, who disappeared, and the sniper.* He grabbed the AR-15 from the dead man and crawled his way over to the entrance. On his belly, he aimed into the grove of trees where the sniper was hidden.

He opened automatic fire into the forest. The rounds tore apart branches, and an array of leaves flew into the air along with a cloud of dirt. Nothing moved, but it didn't mean he'd hit his target.

Gunfire riddled the wall of his home from behind, and he twisted to see holes popping through. He fired the remaining rounds back into the area where the bullets had come from, and something slammed hard against the side of the house and slid down. The air was silent of gunfire.

He quickly moved to the hatch, and gunfire opened again and tore through his front door. *The sniper!*

Conner jumped through the hatch and crawled to where Pam and the boys were huddled. She held the pistol in her trembling hands.

"Everyone okay?" Conner whispered.

Jacob said, "Yes."

Noah nodded.

"How are *you*?" Pam asked Conner while eyeing the bloody wound beneath his shoulder.

"I'm fine." He shrugged, wincing slightly.

Conner saw the body lying on the ground on the west side of his home, where he'd fired into the wall, and realized it was a safe direction to go. At least for the moment. It would put the trailer between them and the sniper.

"Let's go that way." He pointed and led them west.

He heard the muffled sound of his phone ringing from inside the home, and Pam turned to him with wild eyes.

"Your *phone*?" she asked with panic.

He gave a sorry grimace and said, "I'm afraid I left it inside. You?"

She sighed and nodded. "Me too."

DEX STOOD NEXT TO REAGAN with anticipation as she pressed her phone to her ear and her other hand picked at her lip.

"They're still not answering," Reagan said.

"Shit." Dex closed his eyes. He turned to Geoff, who was sitting on a chair in their dining room, wrapping his wounded arm with a new bandage. "You okay?" Dex asked him.

Geoff paused and looked up. "Still alive. A few bumps and bruises. That fall out the window wasn't fun." He chuckled. "I am old and out of shape."

"I'm glad you were here. Thank you."

"I've texted and called them both. No one is answering." Reagan's voice cracked.

"I'm sure they're okay," Dex said soothingly, but deep down, he felt the same level of fear for his family. "I trust Conner, and you know Pam. No one's better with the kids."

"I don't get why they can't send a quick text back. Just the word *okay* would be enough." Her tone escalated to anger.

Dex didn't want to say, *They might be amid a gunfight or running away*. It might have been true, but it wasn't what Reagan needed to hear.

"We need to go somewhere safe. Cops will be here any minute. Not to mention the bad guys will send reinforcements," Geoff said.

"Where the hell can we go?" Reagan asked. "*They're everywhere.* How did they even know we were *here*? They're probably at Conner's house right now..." Reagan choked, and tears ran from her eyes. "And we left our *children*."

"Honey." Dex softened his eyes and pulled her to him, letting her sob on his chest. Then her phone rang.

"Hello?" she answered it midring. "Hello? Pam?"

Dex studied her expressions. The color ran from Reagan's face.

"Put it on speaker," Dex said.

Reagan complied.

"Who is this?" A man finally spoke on the other end. His voice held a malicious tone.

"Who is this?" Reagan threw back at the strange voice.

After a few seconds, the stranger said, "They're dead." The words didn't register at first. It couldn't be true. "The man and the woman are both dead. I killed the two children too. They didn't stand a chance."

Reagan dropped the phone and sank back in her chair. She might as well have been hit by a semi.

AUTHOR NOTES: *I lived in a twin home when I wrote this originally, and so everything that happens at the Sanders home, I picture the layout of that home. I also threw vehicles into the story that we were driving at the time. Earlier, a Ford Focus followed Dex and his family, and before that was a blue Toyota Corolla. Both of these cars were vehicles that my sons had at the time. So now every time I read this, it's time-stamped.*

Chapter 16: The Sniper

Conner crouched next to Pam and the boys, who sat against a tree. He'd led them into the thicket west of his trailer and stopped about fifty feet away at the top of an incline. He crawled to a line of shrubs and peeked over them at his home below. A dead body lay crumpled behind the trailer. The ground around it had turned crimson, and the side of his mobile home had been turned to Swiss cheese from bullets.

The black SUV hadn't moved. His truck still sat where he'd parked it. He didn't see any movement. He focused his eyes on the windows of his home, but visibility at this distance wasn't clear. Finally, he saw movement. A body moved past the kitchen window. The sniper was still in there.

"What do you see? Shouldn't we keep moving and get out of here?" Pam called to him.

"No." Conner turned to her, shaking his head. "I don't think so. Not yet." He held up his forefinger, signaling to be quiet, and turned his attention back to the trailer.

Conner waited for several minutes. He wanted the killer to leave his home. If the sniper left and drove off, it would be ideal. If he didn't drive away but still came outside, at least Conner stood a chance of shooting him. He felt confident he could hit his target at this distance. But he needed the man to be outside. He couldn't risk shooting at him through the window. The likelihood of his missing was greater. If he shot and missed, then the killer would know their position. He wanted the sniper to believe he was long gone so he'd feel comfortable and make mistakes.

The body crossed the window again. *What the hell is he doing? Does he know I'm watching him? That I'm waiting for him to get open?* The enemy was a sniper. He'd been trained with skills. He wasn't going to leave.

Keeping low, Conner crept back to Pam and the boys.

"I have to go down there."

"Wait—what?" Pam guffawed.

"We need a vehicle, and we need our phones. We can't risk him having those."

He saw Pam weighing the options in her head. She never agreed with him, but she didn't fight it either.

"Uncle Conner!" Jacob cried. "Don't leave us."

"It's okay, bud. I will be careful, and I'll be back." He turned to Pam. "You still have your gun?"

She nodded.

Conner set his rifle down. He'd be stealthier without it. He checked his pistol and shoved it into the back of his pants. He gave them an informal salute and commenced down the slope.

Crouching, he was careful not to touch the shrubs and brush around him. If the enemy was watching, he would be looking for any signs of movement. Conner took his time getting to the bottom of the hill. There was no rush. Every move had to be precise. He inched to a fallen log behind some burning bushes and peeped through. Ten feet of open space stood between him and his mobile home.

He could see into most of the windows now. He saw no one. He listened for movement and didn't hear any. If he didn't know any better, he'd think the house was empty. The sniper inside was not giving away his position.

Fear bubbled in Conner's stomach. He had to make a move, and he was terrified of being spotted in doing so. He had no choice. He lay on his stomach and crawled to the edge of the mobile home, cringing the entire way. He sneaked underneath the trailer to the trapdoor they'd escaped from. He positioned himself on his back and withdrew his pistol. He waited for several minutes, listening for any creak or footfall that'd tell him where his enemy was. The air was silent. He watched as a spider crawled along a web above him.

It was a game of chess, and Conner had to make the first move. The trapdoor was above his right foot. He raised his foot and kicked the trapdoor as hard as he could. The wooden door flew open with a startling crash and then slammed closed. Conner quickly pulled his knees to his chest as the pounding of running feet rocked the floor above him. The floor creaked and bulged slightly. He was never more thankful for cheap flooring than he was now.

Gunfire erupted from above, turning the trapdoor into flying pieces of wooden shrapnel. Two tiny chunks hit Conner—one against his cheek, and the other bounced off his forehead. Conner's plan to scare his enemy into making a rash decision had paid off. He knew right where the sniper stood. Conner aimed at the bulge and fired several shots through the underside of the floor.

He heard a yelp and several thuds. Now there was silence. *Did I hit him?* He was sure he had but not positive the man was dead. Conner had to move fast.

He quickly shifted his body around until his head was at the trapdoor and then rose through it while keeping his gun up. The sniper was sitting with his back against the fridge, panting. Beads of sweat and blood streamed down his face. His eyes darted to Conner, and he brought his rifle around. Conner was faster and pounded three more bullets into him. The lead hit his body like it was a side of beef with sickening thuds. The man's body fell slack, eyes frozen open.

Conner hoisted the rest of himself through the opening. He looked down at the man. Satisfied that he was dead, Conner pushed the body aside, opened the fridge, and took out a beer. He cracked it open and took two big gulps.

"Cheers, fucker," he said to the dead man then raised the bottle to his lips and took another swig.

DEX HELD HIS WIFE IN his arms as she convulsed with sobs. He wanted to fall apart, too, but he had to stay strong. He couldn't let his mind go there. He refused to believe that they were dead. They couldn't be.

"Guys." Geoff ran to them from the front door. "Neighbors are getting restless, and I hear sirens. We gotta go now."

"Okay," Dex said and put his arm around Reagan, guiding her to the door. She took in deep breaths, attempting to calm her sobs. They had packed clothes and toiletries into two suitcases, and Geoff hauled them out to the vehicle.

Then her phone rang, and everyone halted.

She looked at the phone in her hand with horror. "It's either Pam or... *him*."

She slid the phone lock open to answer. "Hello?"

Dex held his breath.

"Pam?" Reagan asked. "*Oh, Pam.*"

Dex's and Geoff's eyes were transfixed on Reagan. Suddenly her body unclenched, and her shoulders sank as she let out a breath. "Oh, thank God." She turned and mouthed, "They're fine," to Dex.

"Tell Conner to go to my cabin. He knows where it is," Geoff told Reagan while she was on the phone, and she nodded.

Tears suddenly broke free from Dex's eyes. He thanked God for keeping his boys alive.

"Geoff says to go to his cabin. Conner knows where it is." Reagan paused then asked, "Have the kids eaten? They must be hungry." She paused again as Pam answered on the other end. "Oh good. I owe you and Conner everything. Be sure to tell him and tell the boys we love them. We'll be together soon. We're leaving for the cabin now."

Reagan turned her gaze to Geoff for confirmation, and he nodded.

AUTHOR NOTES: *Originally, I didn't have this scene in the story. I skipped ahead, giving this section a brief description, and left the rest to the imagination. Not to mention the tension and fear going through Dex and Reagan's minds not knowing if their loved ones are dead or alive. But I always wondered what happened to Conner, Pam, and the kids during this event, and it turned out to be one of the coolest scenes to me. In the next chapter is a good car chase and a shoot-out on the road. I always love those. Here you go.*

Chapter 17: Road Trouble

Dex and Reagan sat in the back of Pam's Lexus while Geoff drove. Dex flipped through the book from Wes, searching for any clues, while Reagan texted back and forth with her sister. He reread what Wes had written. *Read this. Keep your mind open. There is so much to learn here. It's extremely important.* He flipped to the first chapter and began to read. He was three pages in when Reagan finished texting and turned to him.

"Men came to Conner's house. They fired on them—they nearly got Noah and Jacob." Her eyes filled with tears, and her bottom lip trembled. "Pam pulled the kids away in the nick of time. Conner got them out through a secret door or something in the bottom of his trailer, and he killed four men. He got shot in the arm but said it went in and out, and he's got it wrapped up. He's going to be okay."

"I hope that one of those men was that *fucker* on the phone," Dex said.

"They left their phones behind. Conner went back to get them. He ended up shooting and killing that guy."

"Good." Dex clenched his teeth, filled with rage. "They attacked *our children.*" He shook his head in fury. "I'm going to fucking kill them."

Reagan pulled away slightly.

He turned to her concerned face and asked, "What?"

"I can't lose you," Reagan said.

"You won't."

"I will if you run off half-cocked like that. I want them dead, too, but we have to keep our heads clear."

"I am clear, and I mean to kill them. It's that simple," he said matter-of-factly.

"Who *are* you?"

He frowned. "What do you mean?"

"I mean who was that guy back at our house? Charging down the stairs with two guns blazing and fighting off a man with a knife?" Reagan asked.

"Who was that woman who saved my life from that guy? And in the stairwell back at *that* place? You saved me twice."

She shrugged. "I suppose."

"We're doing what we have to. Don't let your mind go beyond that."

"Parenting two-point-oh." She smiled.

Dex chuckled. "I don't remember reading any of this in those parenting books you forced me to read."

"It's just... you're a car salesman. And a husband and a father. But you fought like a professional soldier or something. Like you've done this before. Don't get me wrong. I am thankful. But I have to know. Are you secretly in the CIA or something?"

"Really?" He smirked. He gently brushed the hair back from her face. "Maybe it's from all the action movies I watch. I just do what Steven Seagal would do."

She chuckled and smacked his chest. "And I just do what Sarah Connor would do."

Geoff glanced in the rearview mirror and said, "We gotta stop and get gas. I think we're in the clear now."

"Sounds good. I need to pee," Dex said.

"We need to pick up some items too. We'll need food and things at the cabin," Reagan added.

Geoff turned in to a convenience store and parked beside a gas pump. Dex and Reagan entered the store, Dex breaking off momentarily to use the restroom. When he came out, he found Reagan roaming the aisles. She had an armful of items such as cans of chili and soup and bags of chips.

"Let me help you with those," Dex offered.

"I'm okay. You can get some drinks and water bottles. We'll need those."

Dex nodded, and as he moved to get the drinks, she stopped him. "That lady has been watching me this whole time," she whispered.

Dex eyed the store. There were three men, two teenagers, and one lady. None of them appeared to be together except for the teens. The woman was in her thirties and wore her blond hair wrapped in a tight bun atop her head. Ringlets dangled across her temples, and her eyes were narrow behind a pair of glasses. Her eyes darted to Reagan and then to Dex. They locked into a stare until it was uncomfortable. She pulled away and turned to another man at the other end of the store.

Dex twisted and caught the man glaring at him. Then the man turned to the blond woman. *What the hell's going on here?* Dex thought. The man and the woman shared looks. Dex had had enough. He marched toward the guy.

"Can I help you?" Dex demanded sternly.

"Huh?" The man turned, surprised.

"You keep staring at me and my wife. Do you have a problem?"

"I-I don't know what you're talking about," the man said, but he didn't sound convincing.

Dex pointed at the blond woman. "You too, lady! Who the hell are you?"

She froze in her spot. Tension was hot in the air. People in the store stopped where they were and gawked at the scene.

Dex stepped closer to the stranger. The man backed away.

"Leave my wife and me alone."

The woman set her groceries down and hurried out of the store.

Dex placed his open hand against the gun hilt beneath his shirt. The man's eyes followed Dex's hands. Sweat ran down the side of his face.

"I'm just doing some shopping," the stranger said.

"Do it somewhere else."

The man paused and looked at the blond woman standing outside. He turned back to Dex with his hands up.

"You win, buddy," he said. "I don't know what's up, but I'm outta here."

"Quickstep it, then," Dex urged him.

The man trotted to the door and bolted.

Dex stepped next to the teenagers.

The one with long hair said, "Holy shit, dude."

"'Holy shit' is right," Dex said.

IT HAD BEEN TWENTY minutes since they'd left the gas station, and Geoff was back behind the wheel. He preferred to take back roads until he didn't have a choice. No one talked until Reagan broke the silence.

"Do you think they were part of them?"

Dex turned to her. "The people at the gas station? I don't know. If they weren't, they were real nosy. I feel like I can't trust anyone anymore."

Geoff glanced in the rearview mirror, and Dex caught his eyes.

"What is it?" Dex asked.

"We have someone tailing us. That silver Honda."

Dex and Reagan twisted to look at the car behind them. Its windows were shaded too dark to see who was inside. The Honda turned sharply and sped up alongside them on Dex's side. The passenger-side window rolled down, and a man poked the top half of his body out. His silver hair blew in the wind.

"Z." Dex grunted.

Z had a pistol in his right hand. Dex ducked while also pulling Reagan down as Z fired two shots. The rounds blew out Dex's window but missed them.

"Son of a bitch." Dex withdrew his pistol and pushed his head and arm out the window.

"Dex," Reagan called.

For a moment, Dex and Z were face-to-face, only five feet apart. Both pointed their pistols at each other.

Geoff jerked their SUV into the Honda, and both Z's and Dex's bodies shook and fell back into the vehicles. They both fired aimless shots.

Dex popped his head out the window again. The Honda was still in the lane next to them but a car length back now. Z stuck his head out, and Dex fired three shots that hit the windshield and Z's door. Z didn't flinch. He aimed and fired back.

Dex slid back into the vehicle as bullets riddled his door. Shrapnel and pieces of glass showered him.

Vehicles in the surrounding lanes quickly swerved and moved away from the gunfight. The Honda attempted to pull alongside the SUV again, but Geoff maneuvered into that lane, blocking them. That went back and forth several times, and then the Honda pulled back and crept up to their bumper.

Z aimed his gun at the tires of the SUV. Geoff caught sight of it in his mirrors and slammed on the brakes before the gun went off. The Honda smacked into the back of them, and Z lost his gun.

Geoff accelerated, and the Honda followed.

They approached an intersection, then the light turned yellow. As they passed through the light, Dex saw a man in a Dodge pickup truck in the crossing lane, waiting for his light to turn green. He had a round face, his head was bald except for white on the sides, and he wore glasses. He locked eyes with Dex, and a small smile spread across his face.

The bald man stomped on the gas and shot his truck off into the intersection. He barely missed their SUV and crashed into the Honda.

The back end of the Honda lifted ten feet in the air, glass exploded, and the high pitch of crunching metal echoed. Z flew from the vehicle like a rag doll, and fluid spread out on the pavement beneath them as gas tanks and radiators burst open. Car tires screeched. Two other vehicles became victims of the crash and smashed into the Honda, spinning it.

The truck backed out of the wreckage and sped away.

"That truck just saved us," Dex exclaimed.

"Why would he do that?" Reagan asked.

"I don't know. He seemed to know me."

"You know him?" she asked.

"I don't know. But he seemed familiar."

AUTHOR NOTES: *I love putting a cabin in the woods in my stories, as you'll see in the next chapter. It is a perfect setting to drum up horrific events and attacks by supernatural creatures or demonic humans. A cabin plays a huge role in* Damage Inc.: The Hit List *and is the basis of my short story,* The Lake, *in* Tree of Souls. *Friends of ours own a cabin in Idaho, where we get the privilege of visiting once or twice per year. This is their cabin. The image in my head is their layout.*

Chapter 18: Cabin Hideaway

The smell of pine reached Dex's nose through his broken window, and he watched as they passed lodgepole pines, one after another. They'd been driving through the canyon for thirty minutes, and finally, Geoff slowed and turned onto a dirt driveway. They drove for another ten minutes then turned onto a long driveway that led up to a cabin tucked among the trees.

Conner, Pam, and the boys stood on the front porch, waving as they parked behind Conner's truck.

Reagan was out of the vehicle before it had even stopped and ran to her boys then wrapped each of them in a huge hug. She kissed their cheeks and squeezed them tightly. Dex approached and stretched his big arms around all three.

"I love you, guys," Dex said.

"You would not believe what happened to us!" Jacob exclaimed.

"I know. Conner and Pam told us all about it," Dex said.

"We're just glad you're safe," Reagan said, looking at Conner and Pam. "I can't thank you two enough."

"The *thanks* belong to Rambo." Pam hooked a thumb at Conner.

He shrugged sheepishly.

Reagan walked up the steps to Conner and stopped. "I know." She smiled and hugged him tight. "Thank you. Thank you."

"Anything for you and my nephews," Conner said.

Reagan pulled back and looked at his shoulder wrapped in bandages.

"How's your arm? Are you okay?"

"Yeah. Just a flesh wound. It's stopped bleeding now." He glanced at Pam. "She took care of me."

Limping, Geoff walked up the porch steps.

"You okay, bud?" Conner asked.

"Took a tumble off the roof. I think I jarred a few things loose. Especially in my hip." He raised his eyebrows. "Anyone follow you?" he asked Conner.

"We had a couple of cars in the beginning, but I shook 'em. Nobody followed us up here. How 'bout you?"

"We left some carnage on the road back in Denver," Dex replied as he approached the porch with a suitcase. "No one since then."

After getting settled, Reagan and Pam went upstairs with the boys, filling each other in on details and prepping the boys' beds. Conner sat on the ledge of the fireplace, cleaning his rifle. Geoff sat in a chair, checking his phone, and Dex sat on the couch, reading his book.

The quiet solitude gave him a sense of peace for the first time since the family had been abducted, and Dex hoped it wasn't a false sense of security. Every few minutes, he glanced out the front windows for intruders.

"Finding anything in that book?" Conner asked Dex.

"I'm a quarter of the way through, but nothing's jumping out at me yet. It's straightforward, and it's written well. It reads almost like a biography, filling in so many details and backing them up with a history that's almost too wild to make up."

"What's it about?" Conner asked.

"It's about a paranormal research team investigating strange disturbances linked to a lake in Montana. So far, there've been a ton of stories and first-person accounts of weird occurrences, sightings of unnatural creatures, werewolves, demons, and people dying mysteriously. It all centers around this body of water. They're preparing to take a trip there to investigate. That's the part I'm at now, anyway."

Geoff glanced at Dex with interest, didn't say anything, and then turned his attention back to his phone.

"Sounds like *The Horror in The Lake*. Remember that movie?" Conner asked Geoff.

Without looking up, Geoff said, "No."

"Yes, you do. We saw it together last year. It's one of my favorites."

"I didn't see it."

"Both of us and Jaxson went over to Tate and Brenda's place. We had a barbecue and a few beers, and Brenda tried to hit on me when Tate wasn't lookin'. It was messed up. You don't remember that?"

"I don't remember," Geoff said.

Conner's smile turned to a frown. He turned back to Dex and asked, "So, what's in this lake? Ghosts? Creatures?"

Dex shook his head. "No. Something else. There are hints to a portal to parallel world that sits beneath the water. I don't know more than that yet."

"I don't see how that book has anything to do with the assholes who shot up my house and tried to kill me," Conner said.

"Me either," Dex admitted.

Geoff stuffed his phone into his pocket, stood up, and walked past Dex toward the back of the cabin.

"Geoff?" Dex stopped him. "How's your arm? It looks infected."

A dark-crimson circle sat in the middle of his bandage and had spread since the last time he'd looked at it. A droplet fell to the floor. His wrist and hand had turned a shade of black, and his veins were webbed in red. Geoff stopped and turned to Dex. His face was pasty and plastered with sweat, and his half-open, bloodshot eyes glistened.

"I'm okay. I'm going to put some more disinfectant on it."

"Good hell, Geoff." Conner's eyes widened, and his lips pulled back as if tasting something revolting. "I can smell your wound from here. We're gonna have to amputate."

"No one's taking my arm," he snapped. "It'll be all right."

"You'd better soak it in a bath of salt and alcohol before that shit takes over your whole body."

"You've been listening to Dex and that sci-fi book too much." Geoff attempted a smile.

"Hey, Geoff, what did your buddy find?" Dex asked.

Geoff's face twisted, and his eyes narrowed in confusion.

"You know. The friend who was going to research Wes and Olive Chamberlain? Our neighbors?"

"Oh yeah. I just checked in with him. He's got nothin' yet. It can take some time," Geoff answered and then walked to the bathroom.

Dex and Conner shared strange looks.

"This isn't like him. Not at all," Conner muttered.

DEX AND CONNER PERFORMED a perimeter check that started with the main road in front of the cabin. Each carried a rifle, and they scoped the road from left to right. The road veered around a curve to the south, but going north, it straightened out. It was empty in both directions. They'd turned to walk back toward the cabin when they heard the rumble of a vehicle. A red truck appeared around the bend, pulling a cloud of dust behind it. The driver seemed to be in his sixties and wore a cap almost as old, and he looked at them with a crusty, wary stare. Of course, Dex and Conner were standing at the side of the road, holding rifles. It wasn't a common sight in an area that didn't allow hunting.

"*They* could be anyone," Dex mumbled.

"What? You think grandpa in the Ford is one of them?"

"Could be." Dex shrugged.

"Not likely."

"They're everywhere. The police in Wichita, the men who attacked us at our house and yours, and who nearly killed us on the highway. We stopped at a gas station, and two of them were inside. Like they were waiting for us. How did they know we'd be there? They kept staring at us and signaling to each other."

"You sure you weren't just paranoid?"

"It's true, Conner. I feel them around every corner. *Watching* us." Dex scanned the trees and their surroundings.

"You think they're here?"

"I don't know."

"There's no way they can find us. This place has no connection to you or me. It's Geoff's cabin, and he's as cool as they come."

"You sure about that?"

"He's a bit off. I'll give you that. It's probably because he's sick from that wound. He's in more pain than he's letting on, but I've known him for fifteen years. He's loyal to the bone, and he can't be bought. He'd never get in with a group like this."

"What if he was forced?"

"Geoff?" Conner let out a chuckle. "You couldn't force him if you knocked him out and dragged him. He'd die before giving in, and he has no family to hold over his head. It's what makes him good at his job."

They began to walk toward the cabin.

"Have you noticed anything strange about the guys who attacked you?" Dex asked.

"Strange how?"

"I was fighting a guy off back at the house, and he flashed me these... silver eyes."

"Silver eyes?"

"Yes. Like it was a second eyelid that rose and then slid back down like that." Dex snapped his fingers. "It's not the first time I've noticed it. There were a couple of others who did the same."

"Dex, I'm not one to call you crazy or delusional, but—"

"I get it. I think I am going crazy too."

"What are we really dealing with here? What do you know about them?"

Dex paused before answering.

Conner studied his eyes. "Shoot me straight here, brother. You know you can. It's just you and me. Are you caught up in something?"

"I wish I were. Then it would make sense, but no."

Conner nodded with assurance. "We need to know our enemy. If we get a chance to keep one alive, then—"

"I can get him to talk. If not, we'll dissect him to see if he's an alien." Dex said the last part in a lighthearted tone.

"I'm with you on that."

They finished checking the sides and the back of the cabin, and after everything appeared secure, they reentered through the front door and set their rifles down. Reagan turned to Dex as if for an answer.

"It's clear," Dex said, and she nodded.

"Dinner's ready, guys. I have chili and bread," Reagan said.

"It sure smells good." Conner clapped and rubbed his hands together.

"Nothing special, but it's warm and will fill you up."

Dressed in their pajamas, Jacob and Noah sat at the table, already eating their food.

"It's delicious," Jacob said with his lips brown from the sauce. "Much better than the food those bad people gave us."

Dex and Reagan shared looks as Jacob's words sank in. It was hard for Dex to hear his children comment on those terrible events. He wished that whole experience could be erased from their memories. As he continued to figure out what was going on and stay one step ahead of the enemy, it was easy to forget the trauma their kids had gone through. It would leave scars that would run deep for the rest of their lives.

"And we get to sleep in a warm bed tonight," Noah added. "We don't have to sleep on that cold floor."

"And you won't have to. *Ever again,*" Dex promised and kissed both of them on the top of their heads. "Go ahead and sit down, Reagan. Conner and I can get ours." Dex approached her in the kitchen as she spooned chili into a bowl.

"It's all right. I've got yours right here. It just takes a second."

Dex eyed her as if for the first time in a long time. She wore a tank top, and he kissed her bare shoulder. Her skin smelled like citrus. He noticed her eyes filled with uncomprehending love and selflessness, and she wore a smile that said, *Everything is going to be okay*. She was a marvel.

"What?" She blushed.

"Nothing. And everything." He kissed her on the cheek. "I love you."

"Love you too. Now, here's your bowl, and here's Conner's."

"Thank you."

"Where's Geoff?" Conner asked.

"He's upstairs," Pam answered.

"Geoff! Geoff!" Conner called, but there was no response. "Geoff!"

"Yeah?" Geoff's voice came out weak, almost a whisper.

"Time to eat! Food's ready!"

"Be down in a bit."

AUTHOR NOTES: *I read a sci-fi book in 1978 by Alan Dean Foster called* Splinter of the Mind's Eye. *It's a sequel to the movie* Star Wars: A New Hope, *and takes place before* The Empire Strikes Back, *so of course I had to read it. I always thought the title was cool. Other than the title, this next chapter has nothing in common with that book. However, we are delving into the meat and bones of this story. Of all the chapters, this next one is the one you don't want to miss. Secrets will be revealed.*

Chapter 19: The Mind's Eye

After dinner, Dex spent most of his time on the couch, reading *The Mind's Eye* while Reagan, Pam, and the kids found a puzzle in the closet to keep themselves occupied. They sat around the table, putting it together. Geoff and Conner sat on the porch, shooting the breeze, their rifles sat next to them at the ready. Beyond them was the blackness of night, and stars filled the entire sky.

Once the puzzle was done, Reagan ushered the kids to their beds. A moment later, she came back downstairs to elicit Dex's help.

"They can't calm down. They're scared the *boogeymen* will get them in their sleep."

"I was afraid of that," Dex mumbled.

Dex walked upstairs and sat on the edge of their bed. Both boys lay next to each other with the covers pulled to their chins, eyes wide open.

"Mom says you're having trouble falling asleep," Dex said.

"What if those bad men come again?" Noah asked.

"If they do, I feel really bad for them."

"Bad for *them*?" Jacob scrunched his face.

"*Why?*" Noah asked.

Dex smiled reassuringly. "Because we have Conner and Geoff downstairs in the front room with guns that will tear them apart. There's no way they're getting past them, and if they did, then they'd have to go through me and your mom, and then you have Aunt Pam up here with you. By the time we're done with them, they'll be so messed up that I'd feel bad for them. But before they can even get here, they'd have to find us, and nobody knows where we are. *Nobody.* Okay?"

"I guess so," Noah said, still unsure.

"I know so," Dex said firmly.

He continued to calm them down by telling them a short story he made up about a young boy and his dragon, hoping to distract their minds, and soon their eyelids slid closed. Once he felt it was safe to leave, he stood up and quietly walked downstairs.

Conner was lying on the couch with a blanket covering him and a pillow under his head. His eyes were closed, and his mouth was slightly open. "Geoff's taking first watch," Conner grumbled without opening his eyes.

"How's he doing?" Dex asked.

"Still weird. I tried talking to him about friends we share and different things, and he doesn't remember any of it. It's like his memory is gone."

Geoff sat in a chair on the porch, like he had been earlier. He faced the night, and a rifle sat next to him.

"Keep an eye on him," Dex told Connor.

"What do you mean?"

"I'm not sure yet. Just... be careful."

Pam said good night and headed upstairs to bed. Reagan entered the bedroom on the main level and closed the door, while Dex took a final visit to the bathroom and then joined his wife. He crawled into bed, and he opened his book to read some more.

"You getting anywhere with that?" Reagan asked.

"I just passed the halfway mark. It's getting pretty intense."

She rolled her eyes and laughed. "I'm not asking for a critique. I mean have you found any clues as to who we're dealing with?"

"Not yet. If these guys are anything like who's in this story, it'd be the strangest shit I've seen. Pretty wild."

"It's already pretty wild." She put the nail file down on the nightstand, turned and kissed him on the cheek, and slid into a sleeping position. "Good night. Love you."

"Love you too."

She was out within twenty minutes, and sleep pulled at Dex's eyelids, too, tempting him, but he pressed on reading. The story was told in first person through the eyes of the protagonist, Jonathan Quinn. He and his father built a team of paranormal researchers, and they had just entered the Beartooth Mountains and headed for Beartooth Pass. Not far from there, they finally reached Dead Lake, where all the strange happenings had occurred. Dex finished the chapter, turned the page, and started to read chapter thirteen.

QUINN

It was as if the lake were sucking the land to death. Chills ran through me when I first saw the water. It was calm except for ripples from the wind. The dead gray pines creaked as they swayed. The water was as ominous as it was unassuming. The dread in the air was thick. The lake itself wasn't very big. It was almost the size of two football fields, and it pressed up against a sheer rock face. Cliffs of granite overlooked the water, and a handful of dead, broken trees stood inside the lake like sentries.

"What do you make of it?" Jonathan, my father, asked as he approached.

"Can you feel that, Dad? The air is charged," I said.

Jonathan rubbed his gray beard and studied the water. "Let's get an EMF detector going and test the fluctuations of magnetic energy levels. I want to test everything in the area. We'll make a camp for the night. First thing tomorrow, we'll dive into Dead Lake and investigate."

Later that evening, after dinner, the sixteen of us sat around the campfire. I stared into the flames, listening to them pop and crackle.

"I've never registered levels that high on my EMF. Not in a remote mountain setting like this. It was off the charts," Jones said.

"Something is wrong about this place," I said.

"Jeez, Quinn. You make it sound as if we shouldn't be here."

"You getting spooked already?" Greg asked me from across the fire. He was a colleague of mine who I'd gone through school with. He didn't be-

lieve in the paranormal and was fearless as a result. He'd signed on to our group to dispel the unexplained.

"Just a feeling I have."

"I've heard all the stories. Hunters and rednecks have a pretty wild imagination once they've gone through a case of beer." Greg chuckled.

"Six people have died here over the past ten years. All drowned in that lake. Those are the facts," Jones pointed out.

"Like I said, crazy things happen after drinking loads of alcohol. Don't drink and swim."

"One of those people who drowned stood up and walked out of here," I said. "His friends found him floating in the lake. They dragged him to shore. They said he'd been facedown in the water for at least twelve minutes. He was pronounced dead. No heartbeat. No breath. The group packed up and were ready to leave when their dead friend sat up. He coughed out water and then looked around. They said he looked confused."

"Dead will do that to you." Greg laughed.

"He stood up and walked to the truck. The friends all thought it was a miracle. As they drove down the mountain, they tried to talk to him. All he could say were nonsensical mumblings. He was different. One of the men, Kelsey Jenkins, a premed student, checked again for a heartbeat. He couldn't find one. Halfway down the mountain, their friend slumped over. He was dead again. He never came back after that."

"That's creepy as hell," Jones said while staring into the fire.

"The guy hadn't been dead to begin with. That's all. There's always an explainable answer. People believe in the paranormal shit because they want to," Greg grumbled.

"Why the hell are you with us?" I demanded.

"Someone has to have a head on his shoulders. You need a guy like me. If you can convince a nonbeliever like me, you'll finally have your proof. But it's going to take a lot to turn me around."

An hour later, we crawled into our tents and soon fell asleep.

Shrieks woke me up in the middle of the night. I heard cries in the distance. The high-pitched tones echoed in the canyon. I couldn't discern whether they came from human or creature. It sounded like the howl of a wolf but as if it came from a person, and whatever it was, it wailed in pain. Then I heard whispers. They came from nowhere. As if carried on the wind from the mouth of someone far off. It was clearly a person's voice, but it wasn't a language I was familiar with. Becklah, sandi, conchurough. It kept repeating those words over and over again. Becklah, sandi, conchurough. And I felt compelled to walk to the lake. But I was frozen with fear and didn't move. The words continued their attempts to draw me to the water, but I did not go. Eventually the whispers and howls stopped, and I was able to finish my sleep.

The next morning, I mentioned this to my colleagues and my dad, but no one else had heard anything unusual. I started thinking I was crazy or that my fear had created those sounds from the horror stories running through my mind.

Then we decided to explore below the lake. My father and two other men slipped into scuba gear and oxygen tanks. They walked into the water until they disappeared below the surface. They were underneath for forty-one minutes and twenty-two seconds. Greg was one of them, and his head popped out of the water first. He plucked the breathing apparatus out of his mouth and gulped in fresh air. My dad and Mike Felt came out next, and they made their way to shore.

"You wouldn't believe it, son. It's the most amazing thing I've seen. There is a cavern below that goes on forever. We couldn't find the bottom of it, but a strange blue light emits from it. Something's down there. I'm going back in later. I've got to find it." My dad's eyes were wild with fascination.

Greg sauntered to a log and plopped down. He flipped his wet hair back with a hand and stared at the ground. I approached him.

"What did you see?" I asked.

He raised his eyes without moving his head and didn't answer right away. Something had shaken him. He wasn't usually so quiet. Finally, he said, "I saw the blue light. Just like your dad said."

"So are you a believer now?"

"I wouldn't go that far. Something is creating that light. I'll find out what it is."

The three scuba divers went out again that afternoon. They were gone for one hour and forty-seven minutes that time. They dived farther into the cavern. My dad got stuck between some rocks, and it took them a few minutes to free him, and then they continued. They still didn't find the bottom or the source of the blue light. Only that the light got brighter.

Greg quickly changed into his regular clothes and walked off into the woods. He was gone for almost an hour before he wandered back into camp. He approached me as I was eating a sandwich. His eyes were complex with fear. Something deep was on his mind.

"What kind of sounds did you hear last night?" Greg asked.

"I heard cries in the distance, then I heard whispers in a foreign tongue. I'm not sure what they said. Did you hear something?"

"While I was underwater, I did, but I'm sure it's just my imagination. Stirred up from all your stories. When you're deep in the lake, in the dark and silence, your mind plays tricks on you."

"What did you hear?'

"It was nothing, really." He shook his head.

"Humor me."

"It was... a whisper. Becklah something. And sandi... I don't know." He waved a hand as if to blow his words away.

"Did you feel anything?"

"I just wanted to dive deeper. I wanted to find the source of the light. Mike had to pull me back. I fought him. I didn't make it easy on him, but I finally surrendered. Your dad, on the other hand—it took both of us to pull him away. We spent a good twenty minutes trying to turn him around."

AUTHOR NOTES: *Quinn's story continues in the next chapter as Dex reads on. I toyed with the origin of the enemy and where they came from. In the very beginning, and not until a last-minute decision, the Strangers, as I called them back then, were encapsulated in ice deep in Antarctica. But I couldn't shake the feeling of how close that was to one of my favorite movies,* The Thing. *A little too close. After I'd finished the entire book, I challenged myself to go back and dive in. Dig a little deeper and stretch my imagination and open my mind to the callings of my muse. For only he really knew where they came from. I am so happy I did. I can't wait for you to discover it yourself.*

Chapter 20: Horror from Below

We set up cameras around our camp. If we were lucky, we would catch images of whatever had been making those sounds. I awoke later that night to the howls again. That time, it wasn't just one voice. It sounded like a choir of them. The whispers came again from a hundred different directions. They filled my head to the point I thought I'd explode. I found myself walking outside the tent toward the lake, and I heard a splash of water. I shook my head, and the voices disappeared. I saw the ripples from the splash but didn't see what caused them. I ran to the shore but saw nothing. Whatever had dived into the water wasn't coming out. I had a sinking feeling that it was my dad. He'd been so obsessed with diving again and going deeper.

I ran to his tent. He was gone. So was his scuba gear. I checked the camera, rewinding it by ten minutes and then watching the playback. Two minutes in, a tall man in scuba gear walked into the lake. The camera didn't catch his face, but it didn't need to. It was my dad. I immediately woke up the others.

"We've got to find him. I think he went back in!" I exclaimed. I looked at Greg, who turned his eyes away. "Greg, Mike, will one of you go? We have to get him back."

"At night?" Mike looked horrified at the thought.

"He's long gone. There won't be any way to catch up to him now. He's a smart man. He'll make it back," Greg said, but I saw doubt in his eyes.

After several minutes of discussion, I resigned to the fact that no one was going in after him. We'd have to wait. I sat on the shore and kept *my attention on the black body of water before me. Clouds broke, and the moon illuminated the center of the lake.*

Come on, Dad. Come back to me, *I prayed.*

Jones waited with me for nearly two hours, and I urged him to get some sleep. He finally ambled back to his tent. Another hour passed, and I was nodding off. A splash startled me awake, and I jumped to my feet. My father emerged and swam until the water was shallow enough for him to walk.

"Dad! Where did you go? Why didn't you tell someone? Or wait until tomorrow?"

He stabbed me with a grave look and walked past silently. His movement was strange. I couldn't explain it. Jonathan Sr. usually slumped his shoulders and walked with a casual stroll. Now he was standing straight and walked with a stiff shuffle. Every few feet, he nearly lost his balance, as if he'd forgotten how to walk.

He sat on a stump in front of the fire and stirred the coals with a stick. I approached from behind, and he was mumbling under his breath. I couldn't make out the words. Then I heard him say, "Becklah sandi."

"Dad?" I sat next to him. He didn't look up.

"I found the source of the light. I found the bottom... and there is no bottom."

"That doesn't make sense."

"It is a doorway to another world. The threads of this universe are thin in this area. The veil is almost nonexistent. This is where our last stand was millions of years ago. We found the portal and quickly discovered its secrets and benefits. On the edge of extinction, a few of us escaped into one of many parallel worlds. We survived there. We repopulated and spread throughout the lands and have lived there for millions of years since. That world, Xalta, is now on the brink of destruction. We need to escape. We need to come home. It is time to reclaim what is ours. This planet."

It didn't register at first. Not until later did I realize that he was talking about these beings in the first person. As if he was one of them.

"We are the Mochvani. We've spent years trying to come back, but we cannot exist in the oxygen that poisons this atmosphere. The Mochvani had to find other ways. We found that the Mochvani can only survive inside a human host. We've tried several times. We came close, but the vessels didn't hold. The Mochvani had to discover what organs to attach to, what to tap into, and how to adapt. How to be human."

He raised his eyes from the fire to me. His expression was stone-cold. "I believe we have discovered the way."

My face and hands were clammy, and my body shivered.

"I don't understand anything you're saying. How do you know all this? What did you see?"

He stared right through me.

"Jonathan!" Mike called as he exited his tent. "You're back. We thought we'd lost you."

"We have," I mumbled under my breath.

I WATCHED HIM CLOSELY the rest of the day. Everyone did, and we commented on how different he seemed. He stayed silent, for the most part. Jones and I left the camp to explore the area, and we talked.

"Something happened while he was down in that water," I said.

"What do you think it was?"

"I don't know. He told me things about a gateway to another world and a race of beings called the Mochvani, who inhabited this planet. Jones, this sounds strange, but I don't think he's my dad anymore."

"What?" he guffawed. "He's acting strange. I'll give you that. But how can he not be the same person?"

"He talked about the Mochvani like he was one of them."

"You think he's possessed?"

I shrugged. "Something like that."

I glanced to my left and saw a large pile of debris placed next to a boulder. We approached to check it out. From a distance, it looked like a pile of branches, but as we got closer, it was clear that they were bones. Deer most-ly and a coyote or a wolf. I couldn't be sure. One of them looked like a bear. Some of the fur still clung to the bones.

"It looks deliberate. Someone had to have piled these creatures here," I said.

"There're at least eight or nine animals," Jones said and circled the pile then crouched to get a closer look. He gasped and jumped back. "Holy shit, Quinn. It's... It's a human skull."

I ran over to see what he was pointing at. Beneath the leg of a deer sat the skull of a human. It had a crack in its forehead.

I WENT TO BED THAT night with a million thoughts running through my head, and I didn't know what to make of any of them. One thing was for sure. Both Jones and I had decided to leave the next morning. With or without the group.

I awoke around the same time that night to more splashes in the water. Fear weighed down my body like a boulder sitting on my chest. If I turned the EMF on, I was sure it would register high enough to bust the gauges.

I slipped out of my sleeping bag, shoved my feet into my shoes, and exited the tent. I looked at the lake at a horror that chilled me to my bones. My father was walking out into the water. He wore no scuba gear, and he was dragging two bodies with him. Each hand held the collar of a man. They were unconscious and floated behind him on their backs.

He stopped in the middle of the lake, where more unconscious men floated on their backs. He'd taken everyone in the camp to the center of the lake. Why weren't they waking up? A blue light encircled them from below the surface and lit up the night. He pushed the two men into the circle of light then turned as if to walk back to shore. He stopped when he saw me, and we stared at each other for a long time.

"What are you doing?" I called out.

But he didn't answer.

"Who are you?"

Again, he didn't answer, only spread a smile.

"What the hell's going on?" Greg asked, exiting his tent. He walked to my side and stared out at the terrifying scene.

"They're all out there," I said. I had just finished counting all the bodies. "Everyone but us."

Something broke the surface. They looked like black tentacles, pencil thin, and they wrapped themselves around each of the men. I recognized Jones. He awoke suddenly and began thrashing in the water. His scream was bloodcurdling as I saw one tentacle enter his right ear, then one went into a nostril, and a third filled his mouth, muffling his scream once and for all. He began to gag on the form that engulfed his mouth as it pushed its way down his throat. The image of his eyes was burned into my brain.

"Let's get the fuck out of here," Greg said, but I couldn't move, and I didn't respond until he grabbed my arm and pulled me. "Come on. We don't have much time."

He dragged me toward his truck. I trotted to keep up but nearly lost my balance twice.

"My stuff. I have to get my gear."

"No time," he grunted.

"But—"

"No buts! You'll lose your life!"

He pointed at the lake. All the men except for two were standing in the water and walking to the shore. Their eyes glowed a bright silver. They were coming for us.

AUTHOR NOTES: *In the next chapter, everything is going to hit Dex like a freight train and send his mind spinning. Horror, intensity, and action are about to erupt. I won't keep you any longer. I'll meet you at the end of the next chapter. Enjoy.*

Chapter 21: Awakened

Dex's heart pounded like a rabbit's anxious foot, and a shiver ran through his body as he finished the chapter. He turned the page, wanting to see what happened next, and it started with a passage written in larger text than the rest of the book. The words read as if they were talking directly to him.

If you've lost your way and long to find your path back home, let the door to your mind's eye be open. This is the key, and you are the lock.

Open your mind and let me in. For I will tell you the truth of all things.

I am you, and you are me. Let yourself be free by setting me free. Say hello and let me know myself once more.

Something clicked in Dex's head. It was as if a shroud had been lifted.

Dex was ten years old. Jack Bennett had sat next to him on the edge of the bed.

"I have something to tell you about your parents," Jack said.

"What do you mean?" Dex asked as he swiped at his tears. He was still dressed in his Sunday best, and they'd just left the funeral.

"They didn't die in a car accident. They were *murdered*."

Jack went on to tell him the details, and Dex pictured how it happened in his head. He imagined them driving in a rainstorm. His dad drove, while his mother sat in the passenger seat. A truck darted out and slammed to a stop in front of them, blocking their path, and another car blocked them from behind. Then men with guns jumped out and fired a storm of bullets at them.

The memory leaped to another one two years later. He was twelve and stood in his karate gi. Jack Bennett had knelt to speak to him at eye level.

"I need to tell you about an organization I run. It's the same organization your parents started, and I need your help," Jack said.

"What kind of organization?" Dex asked.

"It's the kind that's secret. We fight for the freedom of our race. Humans."

Another memory jumped in. Dex was a teenager. He was at a firing range. Jack was teaching him how to fire several types of firearms.

Dex laid his head back and stared at the ceiling, panting. The chaos of memories swirled in his head.

The floor outside his room creaked. Someone or *something* pushed his door open a crack. It was dark, but he could see two white eyes looking in and the glint of a gun. It pointed at him.

They stared at each other for what seemed like minutes, each of them frozen, unmoving. Dex's gun sat on the nightstand, and he didn't have time to draw his weapon and fire before his attacker could. The man had him dead to rights, and Dex's heart drummed.

Raspy breaths cut the silence as the man beyond the door struggled with something caught in his lungs, like he needed to cough up a pound of phlegm. In the dim light, something dropped to the floor. It made a subtle, dull sound when it hit, and something else dropped right after. The man was dripping. It was blood.

The intruder backed away, and the gun and white eyes disappeared in the dark. Footsteps padded away from his room.

Dex exhaled and looked at his wife, who was still sound asleep. He debated on waking her, but he didn't have time to explain the events. He had to act quickly.

He grabbed his pistol and, pointing his gun, quickly exited his room and followed the footfalls. The stairs groaned as the man ascended to the second floor.

Conner was asleep on the couch, but the chair on the porch was empty. There was no sign of Geoff. Dex didn't bother being quiet. He ran up the stairs, his feet pounding against every step. Dex stopped at the top of the stairs and turned in horror.

CONNER AWOKE TO STOMPING feet running through the living room and up the stairs. He twisted to the chair where Geoff was supposed to be standing guard. It was empty. He leaped out of bed and grabbed his rifle while Reagan careened around the corner. They shared frightened looks and both bolted for the stairs.

Conner and Reagan stopped two stairs short of the top landing, where Dex stood. The boys slept on the north half of the second level, while Pam slept on the other side of the stairs in the loft. Dex was staring at someone or something on the side where the boys slept, and he was aiming his pistol.

Pam approached Dex from behind and gasped with wide eyes at what she saw. Her hand went to her mouth to stifle a scream. She turned and saw Reagan and Conner and quickly stepped down the stairs to stand beside them.

DEX AIMED HIS PISTOL at Geoff. Geoff was at the other end of the room, holding Noah in one arm and pressing the barrel of his revolver to Noah's head with his other hand.

"*No!*" Reagan cried, pressing her hand to her mouth.

Noah's eyes were huge and white in the dark, but he held still. Sweat glistened off Geoff's face, his bloodshot eyes were half open, and he panted heavily. His wounded arm had turned to a wet piece of meat. The bandages were soaked through to the point that the cloth was barely white anymore, and his hand was a darker shade of blue and purple.

"*Put my boy down,*" Dex demanded.

Geoff shook his head slowly. "No. You put your gun down before I splatter this kid's brains all over the wall."

"Don't do this, Geoff. *Please*. You're dying, and he's just a boy. Don't go out that way."

"I've killed kids before. Hell, I've *been* kids before. Now, you have about ten seconds to drop your weapon. I've got nothing to lose here." He raised his eyebrows.

"Fine." Dex lowered his weapon to his side but continued holding it. Geoff's body wavered like a weed in the wind. His mouth opened, and he gagged like he was going to vomit. Either Geoff didn't notice that Dex had held on to his gun, or he didn't care.

In Dex's peripheral, he saw Conner on the stairs, aiming his rifle low, across the floor, through the slats of the stair railing.

"What was in that book?" Geoff asked.

"Nothing." Dex shook his head. "It's just fiction."

"Bullshit. I saw your face just now, back in your room. You definitely found something."

"No. There's nothing in it. You can look yourself."

Geoff eyed him for several seconds in silence as if discerning truth from lie. "Where are your people?"

"Who?" Dex asked.

"Don't fuck with me, Dex. You fooled them but not me. I know better." He nodded with a sly smile. "Your people are planning something big. We know. We have eyes and ears everywhere."

"Well, then, you should know what it is. What do you need me for?"

"You're going to lead us to them. Why do you think we let you go?" He chuckled, but it turned into a raspy cough, and spots of blood dotted Noah's face.

Noah kept his eyes locked on his dad as if to say, *Save me. I'm counting on you.*

"You didn't escape," Geoff continued. "We made you think you did, and we've been following you ever since. We could have killed you at any moment. I *wanted* to kill you. All of you. They wouldn't let me. But now..." He shrugged. "Well, now... I've got nothing left to lose."

Geoff coughed again but harder that time, and his gun hand lowered slightly. Dex clenched his pistol and waited for the right moment to shoot. He eyed his target and visualized where he'd shoot him.

"Get ready," he whispered to Reagan without turning to her. "Keep low and go for the kids."

She took a deep breath and exhaled.

From Geoff's side, Jacob sprang out of nowhere. He'd been crawling behind the bed, out of sight, until he was upon Geoff. He leapt to his feet and pulled Geoff's gun hand away with a growl.

Each of them acted as if in sync. At the same moment Jacob pulled on Geoff's arm, Reagan crouched and ran for them. Dex raised his pistol and fired three shots. Geoff released Noah as Reagan pulled him away. Conner couldn't shoot at his angle—Reagan and the kids were in the way.

Geoff's body convulsed, and he dropped his gun to the floor with a heavy thud. Blood ran from the hole in his forehead, his right eye had exploded from the second bullet, and the third hole in his throat gushed blood. He stumbled back against the wall and coughed a spray of crimson.

Reagan had both kids, and they ran to the far wall and huddled together. Dex approached Geoff, his gun still pointed. He kicked Geoff's revolver away. He was surprised to see Geoff still standing. His body leaned awkwardly against the wall. Geoff's remaining eye rolled to the back of his head, and it looked as if he were about to topple.

Then Geoff's eye rolled back and focused on Dex. His eyebrows drove his eye into a narrow slit, and a bloody, gaping hole replaced his other eye. Lines in his forehead crinkled as his face contorted into rage. He clenched his teeth, and his hands reached for Dex like claws.

He grabbed Dex and ran, pushing him back with the ferocity of a locomotive. He shoved him past the stairs and threw him across the floor of the loft. Dex slammed into the railing. His pistol toppled to the floor.

Geoff stood at the top of the stairs, and Conner raised his rifle and fired a shot into his gut. As if unfazed by the bullet, Geoff turned, grabbed the rifle, and tore it out of Conner's hands. He then pounded a foot into Conner's face, sending him off his feet and toppling down the stairs.

Pam backed away, screaming, as Geoff tossed the rifle, turned back to Dex, and charged. Dex was on his feet again. Geoff threw heavy punches like a drunkard in a bar, but Dex swiped them away and dove in with a front kick to his groin and followed it with a strike from each fist to his face.

Blood and sweat flew as each punch snapped his head back. Geoff staggered a bit but came back with full force and thrust both palms against Dex's chest. Dex flew again, crashing into the railing. His back hit the rungs so hard that it broke three of them free.

Like a bull, Geoff charged Dex. Dex was quick to his feet but kept low. He clasped his hands together, drove them underneath Geoff's groin, and raised them like a forklift.

Using Geoff's momentum, he lifted his body up with his forearms beneath him, and Geoff somersaulted over Dex and the railing. Off-balance, Dex stumbled back as well. The railing finally gave way, snapping like a branch, and Dex toppled.

Geoff's back slammed against the wooden coffee table with a *crack*. Three of the four legs broke, leaving the table at an awkward slant, and Geoff slid halfway off the table.

AUTHOR NOTES: *More truths will be unveiled in a nightmarish fashion, and the true, collective power of the Intruders is about to be un-*

leashed in the next chapter. The image of this scene has been in my head like a movie from the very conception of this story. I spent a long time on this part to get it right so that you can see what I see. I hope it resonates well, because this is one of my favorite parts in the entire story. You won't be able to get to sleep.

Chapter 22: The Intruder

Dex didn't have time to turn his body and land on his feet. His right side landed on Geoff's chest, then he rolled off him.

Dex's face twisted in pain as he arched his back and slowly crawled to his feet. Conner ran to him, prepared to help fight. Blood was smeared on his face.

"You okay?" Conner asked.

"Sort of." Dex panted. He looked back at Geoff, who wasn't moving. He appeared to be out.

Reagan, the kids, and Pam ran down the stairs and halted. Reagan held Noah, and he had his arms clasped around her neck. Jacob ran to Dex and hugged his leg, and Dex bent and picked him up. Jacob planted himself against his chest and wrapped his arms around him.

"That was a real brave thing you did," Dex told Jacob. "You saved me, kiddo. I love you."

"Love you too, Dad," he mumbled with his face still pressed against him.

Dex approached Reagan and Noah and hugged them as Conner stood over Geoff, his rifle aimed.

"Hey, Dex," Conner called.

Dex approached.

"He's still movin.'"

Geoff didn't look human anymore. His head was a bloody pulp, his shirt was drenched in blood and sweat, and his right arm looked like it'd gone through a meat grinder. Geoff rose to a standing position, but something was wrong with his head. It sat tilted with his left ear lying on his shoulder. His neck had been bent, snapped in half, and his head lolled from left to right.

Conner stepped back, his eyes widening, and his jaw dropped.

"*What the hell?*" Pam gasped.

"Here." Dex set Jacob down. "Go to your mom, okay?"

Jacob did as he was told, and Dex stepped closer.

"It's okay. It can't hurt us anymore. It's dying," Dex said.

It moaned and gave a high-pitched, inhuman squeal. Thick black sludge jetted out of the hole in its neck and slopped to the floor. Something black and thin, like a spider's leg, popped out from the same hole, and three more followed it. They turned down like fingers and grasped Geoff's collarbone to hoist itself out of his body.

They all continued to watch in horror as the creature slithered out of the lifeless body and spilled onto the floor. Geoff's body, like a skin suit, crumpled. The substance moved like mud, and then arms and legs formed from the mass, and the center stretched itself into a body. The hind legs planted themselves, and it rose to a standing position. It stood seven to eight feet tall. The sludge solidified into a humanlike form, but its skin was thin, like paper, translucent in a way, and red veins intertwined like highways across its body.

They saw its organs pulsing inside. Some looked human, like a heart and a liver, but many of them looked like a bad set of pipes and chambers.

Its head was smooth and round, and two bright-silver eyes opened into thin slits. It appeared to have no mouth or nose, and its arms were nearly long enough for its knuckles to drag on the ground. Its hands were long claws of eight inches or more. A soft cry escaped its head, then it started to pant, as if it couldn't get enough air.

"It can't survive in our atmosphere," Dex explained. "That's why they hide in our bodies."

"It's an *alien?*" Conner asked.

"No. They are an extinct race. One that inhabits a parallel world to ours. They once inhabited this Earth. In the very beginning. It's assumed that they breathed a different element then, when there was no oxygen. They escalated in advanced intelligence to a point of power that threatened this world and others. God destroyed them before they got out of hand. That's why we believe they became extinct."

"*We?*" Reagan asked, incredulous.

"I know. It's all crazy, but it's what I learned in that book. Remember how I said it'd be the strangest science fiction come to life? Unfortunately, it is *real.*"

Dex turned back to stare at the creature, who was gagging and staggering. It collapsed to its knees.

"Many of them were able to escape to a parallel world. They were able to survive there, repopulate, and build a new life for themselves. They slowly destroyed all other races. They took over and ruled it for centuries. But now something threatens their existence again. Their world is dying, and they're coming back into our world to reclaim it as theirs. To them, we're the invaders."

"So," Reagan began with a question in her eyes, "you got all this from the book?"

"Yes and no. The information in the book was a confirmation," Dex said while staring at the dying creature.

"A confirmation of what?" Reagan asked.

"My memories." Dex turned to her. "Knowledge that was already in my head. I came across a passage that unlocked memories. It's as if I've been hypnotized to forget or suppress them. When I read those words, my memories all came flooding back."

Reagan's eyebrows crinkled as if she were staring at a stranger, and she backed away from him. "They really were after *you* all along?"

"Yes." Dex nodded, and his shoulders sank.

"Bro," Conner interrupted as he stared out the front windows. "We got company."

IT WAS PITCH-DARK OUTSIDE. A slight mist crawled along the ground, and all Dex could see were numerous glowing silver eyes and the outlines of bodies.

Thirty men and women stood outside their cabin, shoulder to shoulder, in three perfect military-style lines. Their legs were all the same distance apart, arms held at their sides and silver eyes fixed on the cabin. If Dex didn't know better, he would've guessed they were robots programmed to act in unison.

"What in the hell?" Pam gawked and shuffled closer to Reagan and the boys.

"What is it?" Jacob asked.

"I don't know, honey. Just hold my hand, okay?" Reagan answered.

Conner raised his right eyebrow and eyed Dex. "What are they doing?"

"They're syncing with each other."

"What?"

Dex turned to Conner and pointed at his family. "We gotta get them outta here." Dex turned to Reagan and Pam. "Out the back! Fast! To the SUV!"

White clouds of air puffed out from the strangers' mouths in the cold air. They each turned their heads in unison to focus their eyes on the SUV, and their jaws dropped. All thirty of them let out inhuman shrieks that split the night, pierced Dex's ears, and shot right through his body to the bone.

All the windows in the Lexus SUV imploded, metal crunched as if a giant hand had reached down and crushed it like a soda can, and each tire blew with an explosive sound. The force was enough to lift the vehicle several feet in the air. It crashed back to earth on its torn-up tires and rims.

Holding their hands to their ears, Dex and his family halted in their tracks. They witnessed the destruction through the side window.

"Holy shit." Pam's entire body shook as if she were about to lose her sanity.

"Son of a bitch." Conner cocked his head in amazement.

"What do we do now?" Reagan whispered to Dex.

Dex didn't answer, but Conner said, "We can pile into my truck."

"No, they'll only do the same thing." Dex shook his head. His eyes shifted from left to right across the strangers. He was searching for a plan, but he was coming up empty.

The silver-eyed devils turned their focus back on the cabin and opened their mouths again, and the shriek that escaped was even louder. It caused a stabbing pain.

Pam crumpled to her knees. Noah wriggled from Reagan's arms and cried, while Jacob squirmed on the floor, crying and covering his ears.

Each window in the cabin exploded, and glass shards flew everywhere.

The cabin walls shook with the force of an earthquake. The wood bulged and cracked, pictures dropped, and the front door flew open from an invisible force.

Dex took two steps toward the door, staring through the opening at the evil crowd, and picked up Geoff's rifle. He knelt and aimed at one of the men in the front row.

The man snapped his gaze at him and gave a quick cry, and Dex's gun flew from his hands. It toppled to the floor at the other end of the room.

Conner quickly aimed, only to find his gun flying next.

True fear set in. All options were gone. *Is this it?* Dex thought. *Is this our end?*

The shrieks from the creatures quieted and finally came to a stop. The silver in their eyes dimmed, but they didn't waver their focus from Dex and his family. Cold air gusted in around them, and strands of Reagan's hair blew back. Dex felt the tickle of chills up his arms.

The chests of each man and woman outside pulsed in and out rapidly, as if they were recharging their bodies, readying to strike again. Their mouths opened, and their eyes lit up silver once more.

Before the shriek came, the roar of an engine broke the silence. Something large charged toward the crowd, plowing through tree branches, and several of the people in the back of the line were knocked to the side. Two bodies crumpled under the wheels of a mighty Hummer.

The silver-eyed devils parted and scrambled as the metal beast crashed through the crowd. It ran over one body and parked its front tire on the leg of a woman who couldn't move in time. She squealed in pain.

Mounted on top of the vehicle was a .50-caliber Browning Machine Gun manned by a soldier in military garb. He swiveled the gun and released a spray of bullets that tore through bodies with devastating vengeance.

Two men and a woman turned and took a stance, synced together, and shot out a shrill sound blast. The invisible force smashed into the soldier's chest and shot him off the Hummer. He fell to the ground several feet away.

Another Hummer bounced up the dirt drive and turned in time to miss hitting their fellow soldier. More gunfire erupted on the crowd from their mounted machine gun. Two soldiers exited the first Hummer armed with automatic rifles and fired.

Some of the silver-eyed men withdrew pistols and shot back. A bullet struck a soldier in the neck, and blood spurted from the wound.

Several black creatures crawled out of their torn-up human shells in a last-ditch effort of survival, but the soldiers seemed ready for it. They turned and fired bullets into the black sludges until they ceased movement.

Conner and Dex quickly picked up their rifles, ran to the front porch, and picked off as many as they could. Two of them scattered and ran through the trees to escape, and Conner hopped off the porch and ran after them.

Another one tried to escape through the trees on the opposite side, but Dex was able to stop him with several shots in the back. The man crumpled to the ground. Dex turned back to the others and fired rounds into the escaping black creatures.

"*Dex!*" Reagan cried from inside the cabin.

She and Pam were huddled close with the kids, terror in their eyes.

Dex glanced back at the soldiers as they finished off the remaining three. He looked at the trees where Conner had disappeared but couldn't see him.

He trotted inside to his family.

"It's okay. It's all over now," he said.

"*Who* are they?" Reagan asked, staring at the military men.

"I think they're on our side." He half grinned and trotted back outside.

The headlights from the Hummers revealed Conner as he stepped out from the mass of trees, gun down at his side. He looked at Dex with a confident smile and nodded. "I got 'em."

A short, bald man hopped out of the passenger side of the second vehicle and approached. He wore glasses, and tufts of white hair sat on either side of his head. It was the man from the pickup truck who'd rammed Z's Honda and saved them.

"Dex," the man said as he stopped short of him.

"Jonathan Quinn?" Dex asked.

A smile spread across Quinn's face.

AUTHOR NOTES: *I went back and forth on designing the creature and how it would look. I wanted to keep away from the alien thing. It's not an alien from outer space, and I didn't want it to replicate creatures in other movies or books. Since there are so many, it's hard not to. There*

are still some similarities with mine, but hopefully they're original enough. In the next chapter, we will follow the Sanderses to another underground bunker. This one is filled with friendlies. Hopefully.

Chapter 23: The Compound

The ride to Quinn's compound was quiet except for the rumble of the engine. Quinn drove, while a soldier sat in the passenger seat. Dex and Reagan sat in the back with Jacob and Noah tucked in between them, while Pam and Conner took seats in the second Hummer.

Reagan stared straight ahead, and Dex watched her profile. Her eyelids pulled closed occasionally. She fought sleep but kept her jaw tight. He wondered what thoughts swam in her head.

It wasn't hard to figure out. She'd avoided eye contact and kept her words short since Dex revealed his secrets. He'd tried to touch her earlier, tried to hug her, but she withdrew. He didn't blame her. It was a lot to process, even for him. She may have lost her trust in him, and the thought of that hurt. He was at a loss for words and unsure how to solve the rift, but he hoped they could resolve it soon.

He twisted and looked out the window at the silhouettes of trees as they passed. Out of the corner of his eye, he saw her glance his way. He turned back to her, but she shifted her eyes in the opposite direction.

QUINN'S COMPOUND WAS an underground bunker beneath a deserted warehouse. On the outside, no one would suspect what lay below. The walls were rusted, the ceiling caved in at the center, and tall weeds all but hid the warehouse. Inside was a cluttered mess of broken equipment, boards, and metal.

Once inside the warehouse, there was an elevator with a sign hung over it that read Out of Order. Quinn inserted a key next to the door, then he pushed the down button. The doors slid apart, and he ushered them in.

Once they exited the elevator, three soldiers stood waiting for them. They inspected Dex's family one by one. They frisked them, asked who they were, and shined a flashlight into each of their eyes. Quinn and his soldiers were not immune to the safety check.

"That's how we can tell if you're a Silver Eye or not," Quinn said, pointing at the soldier who was directing a strobing flashlight into Conner's eyes. "If we see silver in your eyes, we know you're one of them. It's the surest way we can tell."

Quinn led them down two corridors until they arrived at an apartment.

"This is one of our larger apartments. It has two bedrooms, a living room, and a small kitchenette. I hope it will suit."

"Yes, it'll do fine." Dex nodded. "Thank you."

Once inside, Dex and Pam carried the boys into a bedroom and tucked them into bed. They closed the door and plopped onto a couch in the living room next to Conner. Reagan sat in a recliner, bent forward, and placed her head in her hands.

"You okay, hon?" Dex asked, but she didn't respond.

"I still think we should go to the police," Pam said. "I don't know about these people. How do we know we can trust them?"

"We can trust them," Dex assured her. "We can't trust the police. Too many of them are turned."

"Turned?" Pam questioned him. "What does that even mean?"

"It means many cops are really one of those silver-eyed black creatures we saw come out of Geoff. I can't believe Geoff. I trusted him." Conner shook his head.

"I don't think he was one of those things for very long. I think they got to him just before Reagan and I arrived. That's where he got that wound on his arm. I believe he got it from fighting them off. Unfortunately, he lost. Once the wound was infected and continued to worsen, it eventually got to a point that the creature couldn't survive in his body anymore. It turned out to be our saving grace," Dex said.

"How do we know these guys aren't those things too?" Pam spread her arms, referring to the military compound.

Reagan lifted her head but remained silent.

"Because these guys plowed through those creatures and ripped them apart," Conner said. "That makes them friends of mine."

Lips pursed and keeping her eyes on the floor, Reagan stood and entered the boys' bedroom. She curled up next to them and fell asleep.

Dex shared glances with Pam and raised his eyebrows in defeat.

AUTHOR NOTES: *After a bit of a rest, Dex and Reagan will sit down with Quinn for a long talk. Quinn will help fill in more blanks to the history of the Silver Eyes. Reagan is still unsure of who her husband is, and it has her on edge.*

Chapter 24: The Mochvani

After a solid three-hour nap, Dex awoke to a knock at the door. Dex and Reagan were requested for a private meeting with Quinn. Still silent and cold, Reagan agreed, and they followed the soldier to Quinn's office.

His office was large, with a desk and a workspace, and next to it was a conversation room with a couch, two wingback chairs, and a gas fireplace that flickered artificial flames. Dex and Reagan sat at opposite ends of the sofa, and Quinn's eyes moved to the gap between them.

"Thank you for meeting with me," Quinn said. He sat across from them in a wingback chair. "How is your room? I hope you were able to get some sleep."

"Yes, we had a good nap." Dex smiled uncomfortably.

Quinn glanced over at Reagan, who shrugged in response.

"I know this isn't easy. Especially for you, Reagan." Quinn softened his tone, and Reagan shifted her eyes to the floor. "And you, Dex. You're still getting memories back in pieces. As time goes on, more memories will begin to fill in."

"Yes." He exhaled. "A few things are still foggy, but I do remember you. You and Jack Bennett met with me when I was in high school. After Jack went missing, I joined your group full time. You're the resistance designed to fight the Mochvani or the Silver Eyes."

"There's a lot more to it than that. I'll tell you everything. You deserve the entire story. Of course, as you know, the Mochvani are a different species who inhabited this planet long before we did. They were on their way to extinction, but a handful of them found a way to escape this world before that happened. They've lived in a parallel universe for centuries. Thirty-two years ago, they made their way back into our world, and now they want their planet back."

Quinn leaned back, rubbing his eyebrows with his thumb and forefinger. "My father and I worked with a team studying the paranormal activity surrounding Dead Lake. It's a small body of water hidden in the Beartooth Mountains of Montana. It's up near Beartooth Pass. Numerous urban legends surrounded the spot, but it had never been investigated. As we got closer to the lake, signs of its poison were everywhere. Dead trees and plants and no sign of animals. We took samples of the soil and found it filled with toxins, acidity, and other elements unknown to us."

Quinn continued his tale, which reflected almost perfectly the last chapter Dex had read in the book. Clearly, the novel was about Jonathan Quinn and his experiences. Reagan's eyes were transfixed on Quinn, and she appeared to be taken away by Quinn's story.

"I didn't help them. I ran. I escaped while they killed my friends." Quinn's last words came while he choked back a cry. He composed himself and continued. "We found a pile of dead animals that were their first hosts. Test vessels, I believe. Then they tried humans. They finally got it right when they took my dad. Then he killed the rest of the men in my camp and dragged them out into the lake to become vessels for the other Mochvani. I think he bludgeoned them first, maybe with a large rock, then took them out and drowned them. My father, Jonathan Sr., goes by a different name now. He's the one they call Dr. H."

"There's nothing you could have done. If you hadn't escaped, we wouldn't know anything about them. We wouldn't have a resistance," Dex said.

"Sometimes I wonder if it'd be better that way. The fight is so futile at times, and the loss is always great." He looked at Dex. "I think of your parents. Your dad was a colleague of mine. He was supposed to be with us at Dead Lake, but his wife was about to have a baby any day. *You.* They were the first people I told when I got back, and they believed me. We gathered a small group together. I used my trust fund to hire mercenaries, and we ventured back to Dead Lake. We set off explosives beneath the surface and above it in the cliffs. I watched as rocks and boulders tumbled into the water. We continued to blow shit up until that lake was all but buried. Nothing was coming through that portal anymore. But I'm sure the Mochvani brought more creatures through the gateway before we blew it up. I'm not sure how many, but there were reports of twenty-seven missing people in the surrounding towns following our trip out there."

"Why haven't you exposed them? To the media or to the public?" Reagan asked.

"We've tried several times, but their population spreads like a plague. They're reproducing, and I think they've found more portals. They've compromised most of the major media outlets. The ones who did sit down to listen ended up scoffing at our ridiculous story. It's not one easily believed."

"What do you plan to do?" Reagan asked.

"Some of our informants believe they might have found another portal, and they've created a base around it. If they have, they could be moving their kind into our world by the hundreds. *Thousands.* We don't know where it is. They are proficient at keeping things hidden. They hold a telepathic power that they use to communicate to each other, mind to mind. It makes for a very deadly foe. Hard to discover their plans, and when they're in sync, they can be unstoppable. I believe you've witnessed some of their powers."

"Unfortunately," Reagan grumbled. "When Dex shot Geoff twice in the head, he kept fighting, and then it crept out of him. The same happened to the others in front of the cabin when they were shot. But earlier, when we were attacked at our house, those men we killed stayed dead. They didn't come back. Nothing crept out of their skin. *Why?*"

"When Dex shot that man, he killed the host, not the creature inside. They gain amazing strength in their last, desperate minutes of life. Those men at your house were probably told to play dead. They wanted you to *believe* they were. Others may have come and given them substitute bodies, if they made it in time, and maybe not. The Mochvani will forfeit its life for their cause," Quinn said.

"So how do I fit into this? Why was my memory erased?" Dex asked.

"Not erased." Quinn turned to Dex. "Just locked up. We have some advantages of our own, and years ago, before you met Reagan, you agreed to let us use you as bait. We needed to find their base and infiltrate their group. We hoped to end it all once we found their leaders. We kept you under surveillance, and then everything went to hell. There was a mole in our group. We lost nearly three quarters of our force. It was a bloody mess."

Quinn leaned forward and placed a hand on Dex's knee. "Jack Bennett was with us. He hadn't left you. Not *really*. Jack sacrificed himself to save you. To save your identity. They tortured him for days. He never gave you up."

Memories of Jack flooded Dex's mind. He saw his face—square jaw but gentle eyes. Jack had returned two years after he'd left. Memories of their reunion came back. Jack surprised him one day while Dex was practicing mixed martial arts in a ring.

Keep your eyes on his chest, a familiar voice said while Dex was squaring off with his opponent. Jack had always taught him not to look into the enemy's eyes, because they could be deceiving. *Always look at their chests. You can see all their movements.*

He'd turned when he heard him, and his opponent took advantage with a roundhouse kick to his head. As he peeled himself from the floor and shook the dizziness from his skull, he heard Jack's belly laugh.

Dex lit up to see his friend and mentor, his second father, in a way.

"Your mom and dad were dear friends of mine," Quinn continued. "You've suffered so much."

Dex sank back in the sofa like a deflated balloon. Reagan turned and looked at him with sympathetic eyes.

"I lost my family. That wasn't a secret. I'd always known my parents had died. Until recently, I believed it was because of a car accident. But they were *murdered*," Dex said.

Reagan wiped tears from her cheeks.

"It's a lot to process." Quinn looked from Dex to Reagan and pulled half a smile. "You two should get more rest. We're having a feast tonight." The tone of his voice rose. "In celebration of your return."

Quinn stood, and Dex and Reagan did the same.

"I will see you tonight." Quinn grinned, and they exited his office.

AUTHOR NOTES: *In this next chapter, we're going to meet the troops, and Badger is a former friend and soldier who remembers Dex. Dex's memories are still sifting in and trying to find their place in his puzzled brain. We learn what Dex's nickname was and a bit of backstory of a time when he was a mercenary.*

Chapter 25: Badger

Dex and Reagan ambled down the hall toward their room. Reagan stayed a few steps behind her husband.

"Dex?" she called in her meek voice, and he stopped.

Dex wiped his tears and turned to her. Reagan's eyes drooped with sympathy. "*I'm sorry.*" Her voice cracked, and she crumpled into his arms. She buried her face into the crook of his neck and wet his sleeve with her tears.

"Oh, Reagan, I'm the sorry one. It's because of me that you and the boys are in this mess."

"It's not your fault," she said, shaking her head and sniffling. "You had no idea."

"That's just the thing." He pulled back, held her shoulders, and looked into her eyes. "I—I don't know who I am. It's like there's this stranger inside me. A man I used to be that I don't know."

"That person is you too. It's just been hidden all these years. But it *is* you. I've seen traces of it. Fortunately, it was that man who saved us. You're getting familiar with him again, and I'm meeting him for the first time." She shifted her gaze to the side and let out a breath. "You're still the same sweet man I've always known. But now... you're kind of a badass too." Her lips pulled into a smile.

Dex nodded with a sly grin. "*Badass*, huh?"

She rolled her eyes. "Don't let it get to your head."

THE SOUND OF A HUNDRED voices, feet shuffling back and forth, and the clinking of silverware increased as the family neared the cafeteria. The scent of robust food tantalized Dex's senses. It smelled of a classic homecooked meal—some sort of beef and baked biscuits—and Dex felt his stomach growl.

They turned the corner to see the bustle of soldiers eating at tables, walking around with plates of food, and standing in lines. They weren't your typical clean-cut marines. Most of them were hired mercenaries, and they came a little rough around the edges. Some had long hair, scruffy beards, or just unshaven faces. They wore a mix of fatigues, black clothes, or plain T-shirts and jeans.

Dex gave Reagan a wary look before entering the unknown crowd.

"Somethin' smells good," Conner said. "I'm famished."

They slowly walked toward the food line, and various heads turned and gawked. Dex saw one man poke his friend with an elbow and mumble something while pointing his way. Then he caught Dex's eyes, grinned, and nodded with admiration.

He saw similar looks in others' eyes. Men and women alike turned with friendly smiles, or their eyes lit up as if they'd just seen a movie star.

"Are you a celebrity?" Reagan mumbled to Dex.

Dex shrugged.

A tall man with square shoulders and thick arms approached. He had a full head of black hair and a thick pork chop beard. He marched to Dex with a spreading grin. Then he embraced him in a tight bear hug.

"Viper!" he exclaimed, pulled back, and looked Dex up and down. "So good to see you kickin' again, Colonel."

Dex gave him a courteous smile, but it was clear he didn't recognize the man.

"*Viper?*" Reagan asked.

"Yes." The man turned to her. "Fastest hands and feet I ever saw. Sneaks up on ya like a snake, and before you know it, you're knocked on your ass."

"I'm sorry." Dex shook his head. "My memory's still a bit hazy."

"Oh yeah, I heard 'bout what happened. Lost your memory. Getting it back in pieces, I guess."

"Yes. I'm sorry. You look familiar, but I can't place your name."

"Badger. That's what everyone calls me." He turned his attention to Reagan and grinned. "It's really Dexter, but since I share the same name as your husband, he gave me a new name. We fought some battles together." Badger's smile turned down as his expression became serious. "I'm alive today because of him." He patted him on the back. "Saved my ass several times. He taught me everything I know. Especially self-confidence when I needed it." His eyes welled up. "Ahh." He shook the solemnity from his face and hugged Dex again. "So glad you're back, man. And this must be your lovely wife and kids."

"Yes, this is Reagan, Jacob, and Noah." Dex pointed at them. "This is Conner and my sister-in-law, Pam."

"It's an honor." He shook each of their hands. "I'll let you get back to gettin' your vittles."

"Badger?" Dex nodded with recognition sparking in his eyes. "*Badger.*"

Badger's eyes widened.

"We pulled that unit out of a hole in Ecuador," Dex said.

Badger nodded, smiling proudly. "Saved twelve good men that day. They were trapped. I didn't think there was a chance in hell, but you didn't hesitate. You led us down that hill and..." He grinned. "I've never seen anything like it. There were only seven of us running into about thirty Silver Eyes. We took most of them out, and the rest ran."

"Yeah, we did, didn't we?" Dex's thoughts wandered into the past.

"You take care, Sanders family. I'll be seeing you again."

With that, Badger walked away.

"You *are* a celebrity," Reagan said.

"Dad's a hero!" Jacob exclaimed.

"Can we eat now, Viper?" Conner teased.

Z SAT UPRIGHT ON A hospital bed as Dr. H finished stitching the open wound on his face. A jagged cut ran from his forehead, over his right eye, and down the side of his face to his jaw. Black stitches crossed the cut like railroad ties, and his damaged eye was beyond repair. The skin around his right socket puckered inward, and his eye was missing. Escaping from the cavity was the silver glow of his real eye.

Dr. H tied off the last stitch and blotted blood from Z's face with a cloth. Z's breathing came in raspy gasps. Two clear tubes ran from a machine to his back, each one disappearing beneath a shoulder blade.

"You're no good." Dr. H put a fist beneath his chin in thought. "This body is damaged beyond repair, and it puts you at risk. You broke four ribs and punctured a lung, your spleen is hanging on by a thread, and half your body looks like it's been dragged behind a truck for five miles."

"I don't care what I look like," Z grumbled.

"Neither do I. You've always been ugly," Dr. H said good-humoredly. "I worry about your *real* body inside. This vessel can't protect you like a new one. You're barely filtering the oxygen correctly, and some of it is leaking into *you*, compromising your Mochvani. You're attached to a machine that's pumping the oxygen out of you, filtering it, and pumping back in our HTI. Without it, I'm not sure you'll survive. Not to mention that you can't go out in public like that. Your silver eye is showing."

"I'll wear a patch," Z growled.

"Why don't we just give you a new body? We have several—"

"No," Z snapped. "I like this body. I've synced with this vessel, and it's strong."

"Once we detach you from that machine, you won't survive."

Z hopped off the table and stood within inches of Dr. H's face. Dr. H's eyes wandered up and down the *Frankenstein* monster before him. Z's right arm and torso were wrapped, but blood was already seeping through, and his face was a mangled patchwork. Dr. H had done his best to stitch his skin together and cover up the bare holes, but pieces of his skull still peeked through.

Z grabbed the tube below his left shoulder blade and yanked it out. Blood and fluid spurted and ran onto the tile floor. He did the same to the right tube.

"What the hell are you doing?" Dr. H shook his head and stepped back.

Z's breathing came in heavier rasps, and his face turned pale. His entire body convulsed, and squeezing his eyes shut, Z gritted his teeth. He dropped to one knee, splashing in a pool of fluid and blood.

A nurse and an assistant doctor ran in at the beeping alarm from the machine.

"Hurry!" Dr. H yelled. "Reattach the tubes! We don't have much time."

They scrambled to complete his demands, but Z put his hands out to ward them off. "No!" he bellowed, and his one eye cut through them with fiery anger.

They all froze. Z pushed himself up to a standing position, his body still spasming. He lifted his head and straightened his back, fighting the invading poison of his wounds.

"Zenophor, *please*," Dr. H said.

"I've got this, Hepparri."

Z bent over and shut his eyes tightly. He clutched his knees with hands that almost pinched through his skin. The nurse and the assistant looked to Dr. H for instruction, and he gave them a nod.

"I got this," Dr. H said, dismissing them.

Z spat out clots of blood, which splashed onto the tile. After several minutes, he straightened again, and his convulsions had tempered to a low tremble. He looked at Dr. H with a grim expression. "I'm fine."

"Let me at least bandage your shoulder blades, or you'll leak all over the place."

Z agreed. "Where are *they*?"

"Dex and his family? The Resistance rescued them. We lost a good many in the process."

"So you *lost* them?"

Dr. H glowered at him. "*You* lost them. Remember? But don't worry. We still have Gilroy. Besides..." He opened a cabinet and withdrew a box of bandages then slowly closed the door and walked over to Z as he sat on the bed. "I'm sure they're prepping a team to come here. You'll see Dex before you know it. That's why I need you at your best. We need to prepare for an attack."

Z scoffed and gave a chuckle. "They're gonna attack us? That's their plan? Quinn is leading his lambs to the slaughter."

AUTHOR NOTES: *Dex is really struggling with his former self and what his life used to be like. He's also feeling betrayed, and used as bait, which put his family at a significant risk, and he's ready to bolt. What he decides at this moment will change the course in a dramatic way.*

Chapter 26: Should We Stay, or Should We Go

Dex took his last bite and looked at the rest of the food on his plate. He'd barely eaten half of it. It wasn't that it didn't taste good. It was the best meal he'd had in a long time, but his mind was troubled. Beyond the tidbits of memories snapping into place, he felt an impending sense of doom. The intensity of a coming storm weighed heavily in the air, and he looked at his wife. She was talking with Pam about her new job at the bank, as if the danger they'd gone through and were still going through didn't matter.

He didn't blame her. She had to distract herself somehow. Dex just wished he could do the same.

"Hey, they have ice cream!" Jacob exclaimed to Noah after seeing two soldiers carrying sundaes.

Noah turned to his mom. "Can we get ice cream?"

Reagan held back an answer.

"I'll take them. I could go for some ice cream," Conner said.

"Okay. If you two stay next to Conner."

Conner stood up with the boys, and they walked away.

Dex saw Quinn sitting alone at a table on the other side of the room, and he turned to Reagan. "I'll be back."

He stood up and made his way over to Quinn then sat across from him.

"Dex." Quinn smiled. "How is your family? Did you get enough to eat?"

"We did. Thank you. I have some questions," Dex said, cutting to the chase.

"Shoot."

"Why did Wes finger me? What was he doing living next to us?"

Quinn shrugged. "Just to keep an eye on you. Make sure you were safe."

Dex gave him a disbelieving look. "Bullshit. I've been married for a long time. My memories were gone. I was *out*. I was safe. You said it yourself. Jack didn't give me up."

"You may have thought you were safe. I just wanted to—"

"Quinn, cards on the table. Lies aren't going to help us here."

Quinn's shoulders sank, and he looked away. He planted his elbows, clasped his hands together, rested his chin on them, and looked at Dex. "You're right. It doesn't do anyone any good. I moved Wes into the house next to you. I paid a good price for that house. Our intentions were to tell you the truth slowly. Bring you back into the fold. He was going to give you the book, which would then unlock your memories."

"Why?"

"I needed you. The resistance *needs* you. You're a natural leader, you think on your feet, and you have the skills we need."

"I have a *family*."

"I know. I didn't want to do it, but I had no choice. We're losing, Dex. It was a last desperate act. I didn't mean to put your family in danger."

Dex sat back and eyed him carefully. Something wasn't right. Quinn was leaving something out.

"You didn't need a leader. You have an entire army here. You can't tell me you needed one more guy. That I would make that much difference."

"But you *do*. Look at everyone here. The minute you walked into this cafeteria, their spirits lifted. They look up to you. You give them hope."

"What exactly *was* your original plan with me?"

"To infiltrate the Mochvani. Use you as a spy of sorts. We were going to leak information to the Silver Eyes to draw them out to you. We knew they'd take you captive and to their base. We were going to put a tracking device in you, but we didn't get the chance." Quinn raised his eyebrows. "I didn't want to use you for this mission. You insisted. No one could convince you otherwise."

"That was twelve years ago. I have a family to think about now. Things have changed, and the stakes are higher. But you decided to put the old plan into action now?" Dex shook his head in disbelief. "I would never have agreed to it today."

Quinn didn't answer.

"You *used* me. You set everything up for Wes to point the finger at me so that they'd abduct me and my family, take us to their base, and torture the hell out of us."

"I didn't think they'd take your family." Quinn shook his head.

"What did you think they'd do, you *bastard*?"

Quinn jerked back like he'd been punched.

"They were going to kill us."

"No. They would never kill you."

"They killed Wes and his wife," Dex said through gritted teeth. "They gave the order for us to be killed, Quinn."

"I-I had faith you'd survive. Your training. And you were too valuable for them to kill. They *used* you. Don't you see? They *let* you go. So they could follow you. You were going to lead them to us."

Dex was silent. His face heated as his eyes burned into Quinn.

"It's a game of chess, Dex. I kept my eyes on you the whole time. We stepped in and saved you when you needed it. Remember the intersection? I rammed my truck into them. Then we came to the cabin and saved you and your family. *Please.*" Quinn's eyes were glossy. "This game is deadly. We've all lost family and friends, but the bigger picture is humanity. We're losing our planet. We're all that stands between them taking over once and for all. I don't like doing what I must do. I've made ugly decisions, and this is one of the worst yet, Dex. But I'd do it again. I have to make those choices. The responsibility is on me."

"My responsibility is to my family, you son of a bitch." Dex stood up and swiped Quinn's plate of food off the table. It slid to the end and clamored to the ground, echoing throughout the room. Several people stopped what they were doing to turn and look. "Where was *my* choice?"

"Dex, please. Your condition is unstable."

"What are you talking about?"

"As your memories are coming back, it causes irritation, headaches, and confusion. I think a lot of this fear and anger is a side effect."

Dex glared at him then marched away. Quinn exhaled and rubbed his eyes with his thumb and forefinger.

DEX STUFFED CLOTHES into his suitcase with stronger force than necessary. He turned back to the dresser and yanked the top drawer out and grabbed piles of socks and underwear.

"Get everything together, Reagan. We're getting outta here," he called to her as she entered the room.

Scrunching her face, she grabbed his arm and held his attention.

"What are you doing?" she asked him.

"They used us, Reagan. They threw us to the wolves." He stepped around her to the door and hollered, "Conner and Pam! Get your shit together. We're outta here in ten minutes."

"Just calm down. Let's talk about this." Reagan kept her composure.

"There's nothing to talk about. We can't trust these people. They set it all up. Don't you see? It was because of *them* that we were taken, tortured, and nearly killed." He slammed the bedroom door.

"I know." She sighed. "And I don't forgive them for it. But leaving here—leaving this sanctuary, we're going to be walking targets out there. We won't survive on our own, Dex."

"We'll hide. I have a friend in New Hampshire. He'll let us stay there." He continued grabbing items off the nightstands and throwing them on top of the pile in the suitcase.

"For how long? And then where?" Reagan asked.

"I don't know, Reagan. We'll figure it out."

"What do we do for money? We're almost out, and we don't have our jobs anymore. I'm sure of that."

Exasperated, Dex closed his eyes, sat on the edge of the bed, and bent forward with his head in his hands. The pain pounded like a drum against his skull. The headache was so excruciating that he couldn't think straight.

"I don't know what's right anymore," he mumbled. Two sides battled in him. His old self, the commander of Quinn's army, who felt loyalty and responsibility to fight among them. And the new self, who carried the responsibility of his family and their safety. The one thing that bothered both selves was dishonesty. Quinn had lied to him and put him and his family in danger. Nothing was more black-and-white than that.

His mind was scrambled with a million thoughts. The new memories resurfacing were spinning him out of control.

Am I really thinking about the safety of my family by leaving the compound? he thought.

Reagan sat beside him, placing an arm around his shoulders. She ran her fingers up the back of his scalp and slowly raked his hair. It always soothed him. He took several deep breaths and felt his heart rate slow down.

He turned his eyes to her.

"I understand your frustrations. I'm pissed too," she said.

"I thought you'd be bursting to leave."

She raised her eyebrows and glanced down. "Yes, normally I'd be all for it. And secretly, I still am. I would be one hundred percent if the world were normal. But in the past forty-eight hours, I've found out that it's all a lie. An illusion. We can't trust the cops or any of the authorities. We don't know who is who."

"Exactly." Dex sighed. "That's why I'm so pissed. When the group came and saved us and I found my people again, they became the only people we could trust. Then to find out that Quinn had betrayed us..."

"Maybe he was just trying to bring you back." Reagan shrugged. "I saw the looks on the faces of those men when you first walked in." A grin pulled up the side of her face as she shook her head at the memory. "It was as if the president of the United States had just shown up. You give them hope. I do believe that one man, one leader, can increase the strength of others. *That's* what you give them."

"What are you saying?" he asked.

"I can't believe I'm about to say this, but I think we should stay. You need to lead these men."

"You want me to fight with them? Lead them to their base, engage in combat against a force that's ten-to-one odds?"

"No. I don't want you to fight at all." Tears welled up in her eyes. "I don't want to lose you. I want you to be here with me and the boys. I want you safe." She smiled. "But is that really safe? And if so, for how long? When I think this through, the only way to be truly safe is to have you fight and finish this. Destroy their base, kill every one of these bastards, and make sure they don't come after us ever again."

"You're something else. You know that?" He grinned.

"I know." She chuckled.

He pulled her close, kissed her, and looked long into her eyes.

A soft knock came on their door, and Conner poked his head in. He looked at each of them with cautious eyes.

"Everythin' awright?"

"We're good, Conner. Thanks. We're gonna stay," Dex said.

"I just got everything packed."

"Well, you can go if you want to." Dex shrugged.

"Shit, bro. What the hell?"

Dex and Reagan chuckled.

AUTHOR NOTES: *Reagan is the calming voice of reason that helps Dex view what is really the best way to protect their family. Now he leads a group of men back to the nightmare motel where it all began. Things are about to get messy.*

Chapter 27: Gilroy Was Here

Dex leaned against the Hummer and took in the western sky. Black clouds filled it, spouting out soft showers of rain, but as the sun set, several clouds parted to reveal a burning horizon of red-and-orange light. The rays of the setting sun licked at the outlines of the clouds.

Eleven of Dex's best men, including Badger, stood with him on the outskirts of Wichita, two miles from the deserted motel. They'd travelled in three Hummers and parked behind a truck stop.

"I've set up thirty charges of C-4 explosives," Cody reported while approaching Dex. "Once we're inside, we need to place them throughout the compound and push this button on top, and that will arm the explosive. Once we're clear, I'll set them off by remote."

Dex nodded.

"Only problem is," Cody continued, "we have no idea what the layout is."

"It'll be a work in progress," Dex said. "There are three floors. If there's a basement or something else, I haven't seen it. It'll be imperative for the team on the bottom floor to verify there isn't more." Dex turned to Badger, who stood on his right. "Badger and Cody, I want you each to take a team of three. Badger will take the second floor and Cody, the first. I'll lead the remaining two down to the bottom floor. I'll take most of the charges with me. If we blast the bottom well, the compound will crumble along with it."

"Best let me take the bottom," Badger said. "You take the top. Can't afford you getting trapped down there. You got family to think about."

"We all got something. It has to be me because I'm the only one who's been inside. I saw a strange room on the bottom floor that I want to check out." When Dex and his family had searched for an exit, he had opened a door revealing a utility closet and three windows covered in drapes. It had looked like a dead end, but something nagged at him that there was more to it. "Besides, you know what happens when you leave a viper at the bottom of a pit."

"You just hightail it outta there. Don't try to be a hero. Got it? I don't wanna have to drag your ass outta there." Badger jabbed him with his forefinger.

"Drag my ass?" Dex guffawed, and Badger laughed and slapped his shoulder.

DEX'S TROOP CROSSED the plains between the truck stop and the motel swiftly and quietly. The sun had completely departed, and they stealthily approached the deserted building of the Sleep Well motel. They crept along the back side of the building.

The darkened structure loomed before Dex like the remnant of a nightmare. He saw his family escaping the room and racing across the cracked pavement, barefoot in their pajamas. He saw Reagan strapped to a metal chair, awaiting torture, and saw his children curled up in fear on the cold floor of an empty room. He tasted the blood from the beating he'd received and the sting of the needles in his body. Each wound awakened as he looked at the motel.

He'd said goodbye to his family for the second time in three days, not knowing if he'd see them again. They'd escaped an impossible situation inside that motel. Was it all for nothing now that he'd left them again? He had to remember what Reagan had said. This was the best way to protect them. He had to believe that.

Conner had stayed at the compound with his family, and that gave him comfort. Conner would give them the personal protection they needed—but Dex was selfish. He wanted to bring himself back too.

Now, put it aside, Dex, he told himself. *Focus on the task ahead.* He remembered a line from one of his favorite movies, *Troy*. Hector told his younger brother, Paris, before battling Menelaus, king of Mycenaean Sparta and husband of Helen, "Your sword, his sword, nothing else."

The area surrounding the motel was clear except for a school bus parked at the far end of the lot. *That's new,* Dex thought.

He turned to his men, nodded that the coast was clear, and motioned to the bus. Keeping low, they trotted across the asphalt and surrounded the bus. Badger entered the front, while Cody opened the back door. Within seconds, they both exited and reported it clear.

Badger looked at Dex questioningly, and Dex shrugged.

"Keep your eyes peeled," Dex whispered, and they quick-stepped to room eight.

They entered the room with caution but moved at a fast pace. Dex led them to the bathroom. Keeping silent, he pointed at the door in the wall behind the tub.

How could Sheriff Hendershot and the police not see this?

The door was locked, but with Badger's powerful snap kick next to the handle, it flew open. He crouched, aiming his AR-15. The stairwell leading into the compound was empty.

CONNER MET WITH THE guards at the elevator, and they granted him access to the outside for a smoke. He rode the elevator and exited. The dying sunlight blinded him temporarily. He saw a man with his back to him, standing fifteen feet away and talking on his cell phone. The man snapped around in alarm as Conner approached. The stranger's eyes widened as if he'd been caught stealing a cookie.

"I gotta go. Call you back later," the soldier said and slid the phone back into his pocket.

Conner nodded a salutation as he withdrew a cigarette from his front pocket then popped it into his mouth and lit it. He hadn't smoked in over two months. But while talking to a soldier in the mess hall who had a pack sticking out of his pocket, the temptation had been too strong.

"You're Dex's friend, right?" the man asked.

Conner took a drag from his cigarette and let it out. "That's right. Conner." He poked his hand out.

The soldier looked at Conner's hand, hesitated, then shook it. "Gilroy."

Gilroy looked to be between eighteen and twenty years of age.

"Nice to meetcha, Gilroy. You been with this outfit long?"

He shook his head. "About nine months. The Silver Eyes took over my family."

"*Took* them over?" Conner asked.

"During a night raid. Took my mom, dad, and sister. That's what they do. Steal families in the middle of the night, take them to their compound, and let the creatures take over their bodies."

"Good *hell*," Conner said, aghast.

Gilroy shifted his eyes away. "I gotta get back inside," he said and brushed past Conner.

"Good night," Conner said.

Gilroy neglected to respond. He opened the door and disappeared inside.

Conner finished his cigarette and squashed it under his heel then reentered the compound. As the guards scanned his eyes and checked him in, he asked them a question.

"Are you allowed to use cell phones here?"

The dark-haired guard shook his head. "No."

"For security reasons," the other guard explained.

"That's what I thought," Conner said, pursing his lips in thought.

"You'd have to get permission from Quinn. He doesn't even like letting anyone out to smoke. But it's better than having you or Gilroy do it in here," the first guard said.

"So Gilroy went out to smoke too?"

"I didn't even know he smoked." The other guard shrugged. "I guess you never know."

AUTHOR NOTES: *Dex and his team continue through the compound beneath the motel. They separate into groups and begin to set charges.*

Chapter 28: Beneath the Motel

Dex and his team moved through the hallways of the top level with military proficiency, only to find it empty and lit by security lights. They gathered at the large, open foyer that sat at the halfway mark.

"This is your floor." Dex turned to Cody. "Set your charges and keep this area secure. Listen for us coming up the stairs. We may need backup."

Cody agreed and turned to move, but Dex stopped him.

"Let's set these charges to go off in thirty minutes. Can we do that instead?"

"Yeah." Cody nodded.

The sense of a trap thickened the air and sent a feeling of dread throughout Dex's body.

"That way, if we don't make it, we still bring the castle down. But if we're done early, we can still set them off by remote, right?" Dex asked.

"Yes."

"It's a good idea," Badger said.

"Good luck," Dex said, and they broke off into their three teams.

Dex and Badger led their men down the stairwell at the end of the hall. Crouched and aiming, Badger flung the door open at the second floor. Again, it was empty and dark. Badger ushered his men inside and gave Dex a last nod, and Dex led his men to the bottom floor.

The sublevel was a mirror image of the previous two. As Dex and his men moved down the first hall, they were met with the same emptiness and silence as everywhere else. They pushed doors open and cleared rooms but met no opposition. Once the entire floor was cleared, Dex met up with his men at the center. They shared the same perplexed looks.

Kitt, Dex's right-hand man, spoke. "Where are the barracks? Are you sure this is their compound?"

Dex sighed heavily. "I'm not sure of anything except that this is the place they took me and my family. Something isn't right. Let's set our charges and keep our eyes open. Call out if you see anything. Take Hawkins to the far end, and I'll take the south end, and we'll meet back here in five minutes."

He nodded, and they went their respective ways.

CONNER LED REAGAN, Pam, and the boys to the mess hall for dinner. Reagan's face was a wreck of concern. Conner was sure her mind was swimming with thoughts of Dex and where he must be right now. Pam's face was pale with a shade of green, and the boys' eyes were wide and their lips, pursed.

"I honestly don't know why we're going to dinner. I can't eat a thing. I have no appetite," Reagan said.

"You need a little somethin'. So do the boys. For strength," Conner said.

"I'm just going to throw it up."

They turned in to the cafeteria, and Conner felt Reagan's eyes shifting to the back of his waistband. He'd thought he had hidden his gun better.

"Are you carrying?" she whispered in his ear.

"Yes," he whispered back.

"I thought we weren't supposed to carry weapons in here. Didn't you turn all yours in?"

"I kept one. I made a vow to protect you all. I'm not about to break it."

Reagan nodded.

Conner directed them to a table at the far end of the room next to the exit and made each of them sit on the same side of the table, facing the dining hall. He wanted their backs to the wall so that he could survey the entire room. If anyone attacked or something went down, he could see it coming.

Reagan twirled her fork through the pasta on her plate while Conner scanned the room. He was searching for the young man he'd met outside, Gilroy. He didn't trust him. *Who was he talking to on the phone? And why?* He had no family left to call, if Conner believed what he said about them being taken by the Silver Eyes. *Who else is worth the risk of making a phone call to when it was strictly against the rules?*

His eyes sifted through the groups of men. Gilroy was a skinny, young man with dark hair and dark eyes. He should be easy to find. A few minutes later, he spotted him. He sat in the center of the mess hall, all alone, at one end of a table. He was staring at his untouched food, and he wiped sweat from his brow with the back of his hand.

Reagan leaned toward Conner. "Who are you staring at?"

"Nobody," he answered without breaking his stare.

"Nobody?" she asked with a hint of disbelief. She followed his eyes and saw the young man. "If your eyes were lasers, he'd be dead right now. *What's* going on?"

"It might be nothing. Hopefully, nothing."

At that point, Pam had caught on to the conversation and poked her head in. "What's up?" she asked.

He spoke to them both. "Something might go down."

"Does it have something to do with that man?" Reagan asked.

"Maybe. He's raised my suspicions, and the rest is a gut feeling. If anything does happen, just follow my lead and my directions. No questions. No hesitations. Got it?" Conner's voice was calm, confident.

"Yes," Reagan said.

Pam nodded.

AS DEX MADE HIS WAY to the far end of the corridor, he passed by a familiar room. They had cleared it a few minutes ago, and now he paused and looked inside again. The cold, concrete walls and the metal chair of torture that sat in the center made horrific memories surface.

The far wall was a window into an identical room where they had strapped Reagan to a similar chair. The cement wall had slid open to reveal the window, and they'd left it as it was.

He withdrew one of his charges, set the timer, armed it, and set it on the metal chair. Its magnetic back clung to the chair with a *clunk*.

He exited the room and continued down the hall until he came to the end. He had two charges left, and he was ready to investigate the room with the shaded windows. He heard a low hum. It came from the other side of the door.

Kitt and Hawkins trotted over to him.

"What is it?" Kitt asked.

"It's the room I told you about," Dex said.

"Do you think they're waiting in there? An ambush?" Hawkins asked.

Dex feared the same thing, but he had to check it out, so he pushed the door fully open while aiming his gun. It revealed another dark hallway, empty but for an emergency light at the end. The humming sound was louder now with the growl of engines. Hawkins breathed a sigh of relief.

There were three rectangular windows along the left side of the hall. The drapes were drawn open, and a blue light glowed from whatever lay beyond the glass. The three men crossed to the windows and peered out.

When Dex had peeked underneath the drapes before, it was complete darkness. The lights must have been off for the night. That was not the case now.

Dex would never have guessed what he saw—a vast room dug out from dirt and rock. It was an underground canyon filled with crags of sandstone and sheer cliffs. Dex saw movement at the base of the crags. The ground moved with hundreds of dark creatures. It was like looking at a civilization of ants, each one moving back and forth, performing different tasks, not unlike the bustle of a main street in a small town.

There were short and large creatures, with skinny, spiderlike legs, and they moved with the fluidity of liquid. Their silver eyes glowed bright in the darkness, and their arms and legs appeared to have no joints. They could bend both ways.

Most of the beings were black, but some were a dark brown, some gray, and others a midnight blue. A handful of them were thicker than the rest. *Were they* really *the rebirth of the first people God planted on Earth?*

Dex moved his eyes from the creatures to a sheer rock face and noticed that they were dotted with numerous caves. Several Mochvani moved in and out of them, and it appeared that these caverns were their homes. Toward the north end of the canyon was the source of the blue light. A small pool of water sat in the middle of the ground, approximately fifty feet long and twenty feet wide. The water radiated a blue glow from within its depths. *It was a portal.*

But how did they live in this world if they couldn't survive Earth's oxygen and elements?

The low rumbling of engines thrummed from behind the door at the far end of the hall. *The utility closet.* He turned to his comrades, who reflected his same shocked expression, and he motioned them to the far door.

AUTHOR NOTES: *We're about to find out who Gilroy really is in this next chapter. I'm sure you have your suspicions already, so we'll have to keep an eye on him. He may not be exactly who you think. Dex is about*

to discover a section in the compound he's never seen before. What lies behind the curtain is a scene that tells a horrifying future. Plans are about to go haywire both at the motel compound for Dex and his men, as well as at Quinn's compound for Conner and family.

Chapter 29: A Stranger among Us

Dex set a charge on the underside of the center window's ledge, and then they jogged to the end of the corridor. The door was unlocked, and they pushed it open to reveal the source of the reverberating sounds.

Before them sat a mechanical structure that resembled two turbine engines from a jet plane attached to several cords and wires. Vent tubes fed off the engines, running up and into the ceiling and into a giant vent on the left of the wall. The whirling blades inside the engines blew gusts of wind against them.

"What the hell is it?" Hawkins yelled over the sound.

"I'm guessing that it's sucking all the air out from the canyon we just saw. Making it possible for them to survive. At least in that confined space," Dex hollered.

"Shit," Hawkins said, and Kitt shook his head.

"I've got one left." Dex lifted the last charge and then placed it on the underside of one of the engines.

They quickly left the room, closing the door behind them, and ran to the opposite end.

Hawkins stopped to gawk out the window, and Dex tugged on his shoulder. "Come on. We don't have much time."

The door they were heading for burst open, and several armed guards charged through.

Kitt didn't hesitate. On instinct, he raised his AR-15 and let out gunfire. His bullets pounded into the first two men as well as the doorjamb and wall surrounding it, blowing pieces of wood and shrapnel into the air.

Dex and Hawkins backed him up and spread lead through the opening and the surrounding wall in a mad frenzy. Bullets whizzed past the three men, ricocheting off the walls and thick glass of the windows. Two bullets found Kitt. One hit his bulletproof vest, but the other pierced his throat, and he crumpled to his knees, gurgling blood.

Dex and Hawkins dove to the ground and slid against the wall for cover. Dex looked at the windows and saw several nicks from bullets, but none pierced the thick glass. He glanced at the door to the engine room. It was a dead end. Trapped. They had nowhere to go.

The gunfire stopped, and they heard the shuffling of more men on the other side of the door.

Kitt, now on his back, gasped for air, blood spattering from his lips. After several seconds, he stopped.

"Kitt!" Hawkins called out, but Kitt was gone. "Son of a bitch!"

He turned to Dex, who lay just behind him.

"We've got them bottlenecked. We'll kill every fucker who comes through that door," Hawkins exclaimed in desperation.

Dex didn't say anything. He saw in Hawkins's eyes what Dex already knew—that it wasn't possible.

Two objects flew into the hall and landed with clanks of metal, and Dex stared in fear as smoke emitted from the canisters and began to fill the tight space. *Tear gas!*

He rolled and picked up one and threw it back through the door, but two more flew in. Their visibility went away quickly, and the two men held their breath and protected themselves from breathing in the gas until they couldn't. Dex's throat tightened, and his eyes burned. He crawled his way forward in hopes of escaping the cloud of gas, but his head went cloudy, his vision blurred, and Dex passed out.

CONNER WATCHED GILROY glance at his watch for the hundredth time and dart his eyes around the cafeteria. He wore a bulky coat, which was suspicious enough, even in the cooled temperature of the facility. Then he reached into his jacket.

"Shit," Conner muttered. "Grenade!"

Gilroy had withdrawn two hand grenades. He pulled the safety pins and tossed one grenade over his shoulder and threw the other one in front of him.

Conner was on his feet with his gun in hand before the grenades had landed. He aimed to fire at Gilroy, then he caught sight of one of the grenades hitting the floor and rolling under the table next to theirs. Conner fired a shot, but his aim was slightly off because of the distraction, and the bullet caught Gilroy's left shoulder.

"Get down!" Conner ordered his family.

Like good soldiers, Reagan and Pam tackled the boys to the floor as Conner flipped the table over onto its side as a shield. The tabletop created a barrier from the blast, and Conner dove on top of his group for further protection.

The bang reverberated throughout the room as smoke exploded and fragments shot out in a frenzy. The frags from the grenade pelted the underside of the tabletop like metal raindrops, the shock rocking it in Conner's hands.

The second grenade exploded on the other side of the room, and a scream rent the air as a man was knocked off his feet, with burns and fragments cutting up his arm and the side of his face.

Disregarding his shoulder wound, Gilroy withdrew a FAMAE SAF submachine gun from his coat, but a soldier attacked him before he could start firing. They grappled for the gun, and the soldier nearly had it until Gilroy shot a kick to his knee, throwing the man off-balance. The terrorist gripped the gun in both hands and slammed the side of the soldier's head with the butt of it, and the man toppled.

Two more soldiers ran for Gilroy, but he twisted and opened fire on them. Crimson blossomed in various parts of their bodies, and they crumpled.

Chaos reigned as people ran in various directions, but unlike civilians, they were trained mercenaries. They toppled tables like Conner had for protection. Some ran for the exit to get weapons, and others threw anything they could find at Gilroy—trays, forks, and knives.

A tray hit Gilroy's chest, and a fork bounced off his forehead. He turned and fired the rest of his magazine clip into a crowd then quickly ejected and reloaded.

"You guys okay?" Conner asked Reagan while eyeing each of them for injuries.

"Y-Yes, we're fine." Reagan nodded. She pulled her boys to her and covered them.

Conner crawled to the table and peered over it. Gilroy was still reloading. Conner shuffled ideas for the best plan of attack in his head. He knew waiting and hiding was not a safe option. He had to take him out. But he would only have one shot at it. Firing from his current spot was unsafe. It would draw gunfire toward him, putting his family at risk.

Another soldier ran at Gilroy with a knife in hand, but Gilroy saw him coming from two feet away. He turned, facing the opposite direction of Conner, and fired two shots through the underside of the soldier's chin, blowing pieces of brain, bone, and blood out the top of his head.

Conner ran from the protection of the table out into the open. He darted in a diagonal direction toward Gilroy. He knew it was futile to get close to the shooter. He just had to get as close as possible to end this fast.

Gilroy turned to face Conner, and Conner dove for the ground. He tucked and rolled like a professional stuntman in a movie, popped up on one knee, twisted, and aimed at Gilroy, who was square in his sights. He fired three rapid shots.

Two bullets pounded into his chest, and the third hit his right cheekbone, blowing it out in a spray of bone fragments and blood.

That didn't stop the madman immediately. He fired back at Conner. Fortunately, his aim was off, and bullets bounced off the tile around Conner. Conner rolled out of the way as a bullet bit his foot, and he yelped.

Several men who'd run out for weapons returned at that moment, and one large beast of a man with a handlebar mustache ran within in range of Gilroy. With a loud war cry, he fired a blast from his sawed-off shotgun.

The blast knocked Gilroy off his feet and onto the table behind him. The mustached soldier didn't stop firing. He cocked his weapon, fired again, cocked, fired again, and did so a fourth time in a fit of rage until Gilroy was an unrecognizable mess of blood and flesh.

There was a moment of silence. The gunfire was over, smoke swirled in the air, and everyone held their breath until they were confident the horror was over.

"You all right?" A man stepped up to Conner with an outstretched hand.

Conner nodded. "Yeah, I think so."

He took his hand, and the soldier helped him to his feet. With one of his feet out of commission, Conner had to lean against him. The big guy walked Conner to where Reagan, Pam, and the boys were. They cautiously rose to their feet, and seeing it was safe, Pam ran to Conner.

Tears of fright filled her eyes, and with her lips trembling, she asked, "Conner, are you okay? Please tell me you'll live."

He grinned and nodded. "Just a scratch. Kiss it better?"

Pam rolled her eyes and pulled a sly smile.

AUTHOR NOTES: *Dex and his men are captured and they're about to witness what the Mochvani do to live people, and it's more terrifying than anything they could imagine.*

Chapter 30: Captured

Dex rolled to a stop beside Cody. He turned to look at the men who'd thrown him to the ground. They grimaced and backed out of the room, slamming the door. He sat up, rubbing his aching head. His eyes still burned from the tear gas, and his throat was on fire. A few of his men were in the room with him but not all. It was a large, square room. Hawkins was alive and with him. Cody was missing one of his men but still had Jon and Roberto. Badger wasn't there, and neither were Badger's men.

"You okay?" Dex asked Cody, who was bleeding from a cut above his eye and a bullet wound in his shoulder.

His face was white and sweaty, but he nodded. "We're okay. We got caught in a gunfight, but there were too many of them."

"They got Kitt," Hawkins spat.

"Shit. They got Max too." Cody shook his head.

"What about Badger?" Dex asked.

"I haven't seen him," Cody said.

"Did you get all your charges set?"

"Yes. We were about to bug out when we were ambushed."

"They were waiting for us," Dex said.

"They knew we were comin'?" Hawkins exclaimed.

"It appears that way." Dex stood up and checked the door. It was locked. "Worth a shot." He shrugged.

"How could they have known about our plan?" Jon asked.

"I don't know," Dex said.

The door opened, and more bodies were thrown in. A large man fell into Dex, and Dex caught him to stop him from falling. It was Badger. His face was a bloody mess. Someone had worked him over good. Two of his men, Shields and Bing, were alive, but he was missing a man too.

Armed soldiers filed in, followed by Dr. H and Z. Z's steel eyes cut into Dex. The crooked scar down his face and the missing eye gave him an even more menacing look.

"Badger, you okay?" Dex asked.

His friend pulled himself to his feet. "Fantastic," he answered sarcastically and spat blood.

Dr. H's face remained stone cold, and he had his hands folded behind him.

"Good to see you again," Dr. H said to Dex.

"Dr. Frankenstein." Dex turned his eyes to Z and with a nod said, "And his monster."

Z continued to bore his hatred into Dex.

"It's good of you to join us. We've been waiting for you," Dr. H said.

"How did you know we were coming?" Hawkins asked.

Dr. H chuckled. "You humans are so easy to figure out. But... we had extra help from our informant." Dr. H approached Dex with a smug smile. "He's likely decimating your compound as we speak." He stared into Dex's eyes as if waiting for a reaction, but Dex locked his jaw and held it back. "And your family." Dr. H's words came out slow, and he continued to search Dex's eyes for a reaction of any kind. "We slipped him in at the cabin massacre. You guys didn't suspect a thing."

"That's good," Dex said with a positive arc in his tone that made Dr. H cock his head and scrunch his eyebrows. "We knew you were coming. We set a trap. We're likely decimating *your* men as we speak."

Dr. H waited a moment before replying. "Nice try, Mr. Sanders. That's highly unlikely."

Dr. H turned as the door opened, and more men shuffled in. *Two cops!* Sheriff Hendershot was one of them.

"Hendershot," Dex growled.

The sheriff met Dex's eyes, and a greasy smile spread across his face. "Havin' fun?" he asked.

One of the officers held a bulky sack, and he lifted it and said, "I got them all."

"Did you deactivate them?" Z asked.

The officer looked confused and didn't answer.

"Turn them off?" Z emphasized.

"Oh yes, they won't go off now."

"Good," Dr. H said and fixed his gaze on Dex. "I guess we won't be blowing up anytime soon."

Dex snapped his right fist into Dr. H's face, knocking him back. Z jumped in with an uppercut to Dex's stomach and a solid hook to the side of his head. Dex went down, and his vision blurred. Z stepped forward, preparing to kick Dex while he was down, but Dr. H stopped him.

"Don't. I need him conscious. I *want* him awake."

Dex sat up, rubbing his head. Dr. H stood over him, glowering.

"Beyond that door," Dr. H said, pointing at a door with a large window next to it that was covered by a black drape, "is *our* world. Sort of. There's a doorway to *Xalta*, and we've been able to bring a significant number through. I believe you saw it through the windows. It's where we get to be our true selves. Your oxygen doesn't exist in there. You will die in that space, just as we would die in yours. Soon we will be able to change all the world's atmosphere to fit our needs. When that is done, your race, your *human stench*, your ridiculous-looking plant material, and all creatures will be extinct."

"That's not God's plan. He wiped you out the first time. He'll do it again," Dex said.

"*God?* That's not God. *We* are God." Dr. H stepped to the window and drew open the curtain. His eyes turned to Z. "There are several Mochvani who need bodies. Let's give them some." He smiled and turned to Hendershot with a nod.

The sheriff turned to his officer. "Bring them in."

The officer set the bag down and exited the room. A minute later, he and three other officers ushered a group of men and women into the room. Five women and seven men shuffled past Dex. They ranged from midtwenties to midthirties, and all of them held a mixture of fear and confusion in their eyes. Except for one man. His burned with rage.

The bus parked outside, Dex thought. *They used it to transport these people.*

The people slowed to a stop as if unsure of where to go. The officers butted their rifles into their backs and kicked at them until they were pushed into a tight group against the opposite wall. They stood next to the door to the other world.

An officer opened the door, and they began shoving the group of innocents through the opening one after the other. Dex felt a change of atmosphere, as if all the air had been sucked out of the room. He stared in horror as the people reacted to the atmosphere change and quickly fought against the officers.

The officers pushed, shoved, and kicked all of them through. The man with rage in his eyes leaped at his attacker. He grabbed for his gun and headbutted him. One of the other officers stepped in quickly and shot the man in the head with his pistol. Blood sprayed over the wall, and the man crumpled to the floor.

Z marched to the officer with the pistol and snatched it out of his hand. The officer gawked at him, and Z pounded an uppercut to his stomach, and the cop doubled over.

"You took out one of our bodies!" Z yelled through gritted teeth. He backhanded the man across his temple with the pistol and shoved him out the door.

"He's one of my men!" Hendershot shouted at Z.

Z snapped his head around to Hendershot. "Now he's one of *ours*. Do you want to join him?"

Hendershot stood in his spot without an answer. The group of people ran back to the door in desperation, but Z slammed the door shut and locked it. Oxygen slowly filled the room again.

"What are you going to do to them?" Dex hissed.

"See for yourself." Dr. H gestured to the window with a proud grin.

Dex and his men crowded around the window. They watched as the men and women all scrambled for life. It was a horrific scene to witness. Humans' lives were being snuffed out right in front of him, and there was nothing he could do. He saw a woman clawing at her throat and gasping for air. Another person scratched at the ground and then began pounding it with his fists, kicking dirt clouds into the air. Others hammer-fisted the door, begging for them to be let in.

The scene turned grisly as several Mochvani creatures approached the dying humans. One woman lay on the ground, unmoving. Her long blond hair splayed about her head, her mouth hung open, and her eyes stared at nothing. A slinky black creature hovered over her body. Its arm stretched and lengthened into a thin, sharp appendage and dove into her ear. Its other arm did the same but entered her open mouth, and the thing began pouring its liquid self into her body. Her corpse shuddered and bulged as the intruder entered and filled the empty host.

Dex was sick to his stomach. It was the ghastliest sight he'd witnessed, and shivers tickled his arms and neck as he realized his own fate. He twisted to face Dr. H, who wore a grin. He wanted to say something, but any word would be futile. His fury made him want to strangle and beat the man to death, but he'd be killed the moment his hands reached Dr. H.

"This is *our* race. This is *our* world, Dex. You don't belong here," Dr. H said.

Z chuckled.

"Fucking sick bastards," Badger snarled and turned away from the window.

Cody moved his eyes off the scene as well and stared at the ground, awestruck. Body trembling, Hawkins stepped away.

It took less than ten minutes before they heard a new knock at the door. It was not the desperate pounding it had been before but a soft, nonurgent tap. Hendershot took a deep breath and opened it.

Dex watched as the group of men and women reentered the room. He looked at the blond woman he'd seen die. She walked past him with an awkward stride. Her feet shuffled and tripped against the floor, and her knees buckled. She caught herself before tumbling and wore a strange look on her face. *She's getting used to her new body.*

The entire group shambled through the room and out the opposite door into the compound. Sheriff Hendershot turned his gaze down as his sacrificed officer hobbled past. He slammed the door behind the last of them. Hendershot kept silent as he followed the line of new people out of the room, and the door shut behind him.

"YOUR TURN." DR. H GESTURED to Dex.

"Can't we just kill him?" Z asked H. "I can't stand to look at his face—even once he's one of us."

"We can't afford to waste any vessels. Soon we won't *have* to use them."

"I can't wait," Z grumbled.

Dex locked eyes with his men. Badger shook his head as if saying, *No, I'm not going this way.*

Dr. H crossed the room and opened the door. The armed soldiers grabbed Dex and his men and herded them through the opening. They fought and grappled with their captors, but there was too much force against them.

Badger grabbed one man's rifle, tore it from his hands, and fired a round into the man's head. He aimed the rifle at another and fired, but Z leaped across the room and slammed an elbow into his temple. Badger fell back against the wall, and Z slammed two more elbow blows into his head and snatched his weapon away.

One soldier kicked Dex in the stomach and raked his head with the butt of his rifle. Dex stumbled out the door into an arid, airless space. He quickly jumped back into the room and gulped as much air into his lungs as he could before Z shoved him back outside.

He fell to the ground and rolled in the dirt. Once all his men were with him, Dr. H, Z, and their guards exited the space through the door and shut it.

Dex took in his surroundings. The cracked canyon walls stood all around them. Suddenly, several Mochvani scrambled toward them. Tall, fluidlike creatures with silver eyes stood like hungry beasts waiting for their prey to die.

It was silent, dank, and hot in the underground space. There was no wind. No oxygen to breathe. It was a surreal, frightening feeling. Dex saw the fear in his men's eyes. The same fear he felt. He only had seconds left before he'd have to let his breath go and suffocate to death.

AUTHOR NOTES: *Creating the world of the Mochvani was a fun stretch of the imagination. How did they live, what did they look like, and are they similar to humans? I wanted to make them as different from us as possible, and yet functional. I'm satisfied with what turned out, and I hope you are too. Dex and his men are inside the Mochvani's world—absent of oxygen—and they couldn't be closer to death.*

Chapter 31: Last Breath

Conner's foot was on fire. He limped his way to the dead mole, a pool of blood spreading around him. Two soldiers were bent over Gilroy, checking his eyes.

"Who is he?" Conner asked.

The large man with the shotgun answered, "He's *not* a Silver Eye."

"He's not?" Conner's face contorted. "I don't get it."

"He's a spy for them. They turned him," the soldier said.

The smaller soldier interjected, "It happens a lot. The Silver Eyes prey on the weak. The victims who've lost family or friends. They promise them wealth. Sometimes power. Whatever it takes to get them on their side. It doesn't take much when everything else is hopeless."

"That's terrible," Pam said, stepping next to Conner.

"I don't recognize this guy." The big man gestured to the dead traitor. "He's new."

"He could have snuck into our group as we were coming into the compound. Or back at the cabin. There was so much chaos that it would have been easy," the other soldier said.

A thought crept into Conner's head, and dread sank into the bottom of his gut.

"Then he knew about our attack on their base." Conner thought of Dex, his eyes widened, and he turned to Reagan.

Her hand flew to her mouth, and she began to shake. The Silver Eyes would be waiting for Dex and his men.

An explosion rang out from deeper in the compound. It was followed by another. Conner turned to the mercenaries.

"That came from the entrance. They've infiltrated us!" the big guy exclaimed. "Everyone, arm yourselves and protect your stations!"

"I need a bigger weapon," Conner said.

"Follow me," the soldier responded.

Limping and leaving a trail of blood, Conner led Reagan, Pam, and the boys out of the cafeteria and followed the large soldier as gunfire erupted far behind them. The soldier led them into the armory and then quickly ran to help his troops. The room was lined with rifles and handguns of all types as well as grenades, bullets, and knives. Conner snatched an AR-15, checked its magazine, and picked up a backup mag, a knife, and two hand grenades. Reagan grabbed a pistol, but Pam refused.

"Come on," Conner directed his family. They moved down the hall and into their room as more gunfire echoed, and two bullets ricocheted close by.

Conner shut and locked the door. "Over there. Behind the couch."

He pointed, and they huddled on the floor behind the sofa. Conner found a spot near them, lay on his stomach, and aimed his rifle at the door.

Whatever comes through that door is going to die, Conner thought. *I don't care how many bust in. I will unload all my bullets, and then I'll start stabbing our way to safety.*

THE VEINS IN DEX'S throat bulged as he held his last breath. He glanced at his men, who were doing the same. Jon's eyes rolled into the back of his head, his mouth dropped open, and he collapsed. A creature approached Jon, stretching a long tentacle arm toward his ear. *He's about to take over his body.*

Dex looked up and saw the large windows above him, where they had once stood and looked out into the canyon. Next to it sat large vents mounted in the wall that sucked the oxygen out of the space.

Dex crawled to Cody, whose eyes were squinted shut, and his body was convulsing. He reached for Cody's breast pocket, but Cody twisted away from him. Then Cody opened his eyes and saw Dex. He must have realized what Dex was trying to do, because he reached into his pocket and withdrew the remote device to the explosives. He handed it to Dex.

The explosives could be nearby. They could be sitting in the room on the other side of the door. If that was the case, the explosives would surely kill them as well. But he would blow up as many of the fuckers as he could.

He fixed his eyes on his men, who locked eyes with him. He wished he could speak to them and apologize for leading them into a trap. He should have anticipated it. What he saw in their eyes was not condemnation but agreement. They were prepared to die and take down as many as they could with them. Cody pursed his lips, Badger nodded, and the other two gritted their teeth and jerked single nods. Dex pushed the button.

DR. H HEARD A CLICKING sound behind him. His eyes widened as he turned to shout at his guards. The man with the bag of charges was at the other end of the hall with three other guys.

They were yammering about something unrelated, and the soldier looked down at his bag.

Every charge in the bag exploded in rapid succession. The men who were in proximity were torn to shreds. Blood, bone, and fragments of their bodies flew and sprayed across the hallway along with flashing fire and smoke. Doors and walls along the hallway exploded along with them. Gaping holes cracked open in the floor, and men flew.

Z stood next to H, and the force propelled their bodies into the air and through a wall. They tumbled into a table and chairs and crashed to the ground. Broken glass and shrapnel showered them.

THE EXPLOSIONS RANG like bells in a celebration for Dex and his men. The ground rumbled, and the cliffs shook and cracked. Pieces of rock broke off and crumbled. A giant crack split through a canyon wall next to them, and smoke and debris blew from it.

Then the vents above them blew out in a flash and a cloud of smoke, and the turbine engines behind them exploded, flinging giant pieces of metal everywhere. The blades of a fan the size of a plane propeller flew through the opening in the wall and tumbled toward Dex and his men.

Dex rolled into Cody as the propeller hit the ground and spun. The blades tore through six of the standing silver-eyed creatures. Dark pieces of their flesh burst, heads rolled, arms flew, and their legs, now attached to nothing, toppled.

The cops had missed the explosive Dex set on the turbine engine. Oxygen flooded into the canyon, but it still wasn't enough for them to breathe just yet. Dex's eyes fluttered, his vision blurred, and he couldn't hold on anymore. His world went black.

AUTHOR NOTES: *Dex set off the explosives, and oxygen is filling the space again, but is it in time to save Dex and his men? I'm sure you're aching to find out, so I won't keep you.*

Chapter 32: Chaos

Conner and the family sat in the dark, behind the sofa, listening to the muffled sounds of war raging outside. Gunfire and exploding grenades rocked the compound, and the walls around them shook. Cries from dying men and soldiers shouting commands rang out.

Conner finished wrapping his injured foot with medical gauze and tape. He glanced at the boys, who were huddled between their mom and Pam, eyes wide with fear. Pam kept her eyes shut as she laid a protective arm over them, but Reagan's gaze was fixed on Conner.

"It's going to be okay. We're safe in here," Conner said with confidence.

"But are we winning out there?" Pam asked.

"Without a doubt. They're coming through one small entrance. Our men have them bottlenecked. They can pick them off like fish in a barrel. And we have good men here. They know what they're doing."

Reagan mouthed, "Thank you," to him, and he gave her a cool grin.

A THOUSAND SHRILL CRIES woke Dex. He opened his eyes. He was breathing in air. It wasn't much, and his heart and lungs ached for more as he sucked it in desperately. His breathing was raspy, and he lacked strength. He rolled to his side. Cody was doing better than he was. Crouched over Jon, Cody was performing mouth-to-mouth to revive him.

Dex rose to his knees and looked around. Amid the smoke and falling debris, hundreds of Mochvani creatures scrambled in panic and filled the air with their dying screeches. Their bodies sank like deflated balloons as they slowly suffocated.

Dex closed his eyes and focused on inhaling and exhaling with more control. Once he had a constant rhythm of breathing, and his heart rate slowed to a normal pace, he moved to each man to check on him.

Dozens of Silver Eyes ran for the door, which was blown off its hinges now. They flooded the compound but found no solace. The creatures continued to convulse with a tremendous force until their bodies finally gave out. Emptied of life, they collapsed.

"What the hell happened?" Badger asked Dex. "Are we *really* alive?"

"Yes, we made it. Cody's explosives blew a giant hole in this place."

Dex walked into the center of the canyon to check the damage. Rocks continued to roll and crumble from the high cliffs, and giant boulders and debris covered the area. Several boulders sat inside the pool of water, nearly covering it. A large piece cracked and broke from a cliff nearby. It toppled onto the boulders already in the water, and with a tremendous crash, it rocked the ground beneath their feet. Dex's legs shook from the tremor, and water splashed from the outer edges of the pool. The weight of the rock pushed the other boulders deeper, and the glowing blue light went out like a candle being snuffed. Satisfied, Dex turned and walked back to his men.

Dex heard coughing. Jon had been revived and was breathing again. Cody sat back with a sigh of relief.

"So, what are we waitin' for?" Badger asked. "Let's kill these bastards."

STEPPING OVER DEAD Mochvani bodies, Dex led his men through the gaping hole that had once been a door. The room smoldered from remnants on fire, and the walls were blackened and cracked.

Two guards who'd been posted in the room lay dead among the rubble. Dex's soldiers stepped over broken pieces of wall and brick and into the outer hall. Wires hung from the blown-apart recessed ceiling, sparks popped, smoke snaked its way through, in search of an exit, water gushed from broken pipes, and light flashed from electricity that kept shorting out. Halfway down the hall was an immense hole in the ceiling. A pile of debris sat below it. Dex halted his men there.

Cody stepped on top of the pile of drywall and wood and said, "Give me a boost."

Badger obliged.

Cody set one foot on his clasped hands and jumped up through the hole. "Holy shit!" he exclaimed.

"Is it clear?" Dex asked.

"Yes, it's clear. I just slipped in a pool of blood and brains. I think this is where the bombs went off."

The men helped one another through the hole until they were all together on the next level. Splashes of blood mixed with black carbon stains covered what remained of the walls, and they found burnt pieces of flesh and body parts throughout the corridor. They cautiously moved toward the stairwell at the opposite end.

Their shoes crunched against broken glass, and they covered their noses and mouths with their shirts to keep out the smoke and the acrid stench of scorched flesh. Dex's eyes burned from the fumes, but that wasn't the worst of his worries. They were unarmed. They had yet to come across a stash of weapons. They searched dilapidated rooms as they went but found nothing.

They weren't meeting any resistance, and Dex didn't hear any sound except for the pop of sparks and the crackle of fire. *Where are they?* He knew there were more men. The explosion couldn't have killed them all. The air was ominous and heavy with dread.

They stepped into another room, which was filled with desks and computers. The furniture was disheveled and covered in dust and particles. Dex saw legs lying on the floor, but the body they belonged to was hidden behind a turned-over desk. Dex warily approached. It was Sheriff Hendershot. The entire left side of his face and body had been torn apart and blistered. In his right hand sat a .357 Magnum revolver. Dex picked it up and inspected it. The gun was fully loaded. He searched for replacement bullets in Hendershot's pockets but found none.

One of his officers lay crumpled on the floor beside him. He had a shotgun, which Badger quickly snatched up. Cody wore a look of disappointment that there were no more weapons.

"Don't worry," Badger said to Cody. "I'll protect ya."

Cody rolled his eyes, and they commenced to the end of the hall. The door to the stairs was warped and unopenable. Badger lifted a foot to kick it open, when gunshots cracked the silence. Badger's leg shuddered from the hit of a bullet, and three more rounds pounded into him, and he fell to the floor.

Dex crouched and fired two shots in the direction of the gunfire. He only had six rounds, so he had to be careful. There was an office next to the stairwell. The door, a window, and most of its wall had caved in. A tall brute of a man marched through the smoke of the interior, firing his semiautomatic pistol. His face and most of his body were painted with blood and burns and blackened from soot. Almost all his silver hair was singed away, leaving a red, swollen scalp. Z's one good eye darted over to Dex, and he turned to shoot.

Dex fired first and caught Z in the chest and arm. It didn't stop him.

Badger grunted in pain and handed his shotgun to Cody, who then leaped over him to fire at Z, but the muscle-bound man was too quick. He dove into Cody with a raised knee, slamming into his stomach, and then Z finished knocking him away with a series of punches. Hawkins attacked Z, but the bastard already had Cody's shotgun in his hand. The blast rocked Hawkins off his feet as the pellets opened his chest.

Dex stepped in fast, smashing the butt of his gun against Z's elbow. Dex grabbed Z's wrist and continued smashing the revolver against his elbow and wrist until the shotgun dropped to the floor, then he punched Z's nose with the butt of his pistol. Blood shot out, and Z's head snapped back.

Dex's blows didn't seem to affect the enraged beast, who snarled and thrust a kick to Dex's chest. Dex flew through the air for several feet. Jon and the other men jumped into the fray, but Z opened his mouth wide, and an intense, shrill shriek escaped. It was the inhuman cry of the Mochvani. Dex remembered the group of Silver Eyes outside Geoff's cabin. Their shrieks in unison had damaged their vehicles and cabin and nearly killed them. Z was using that same sound as a weapon. Jon and the other three mercenaries were blown off their feet by the unseen force.

Cody crawled and picked up the shotgun and raised it to fire. Z snapped his head around to Cody and opened his mouth again. He released another force of sound at Cody, and the shotgun cracked and exploded in his hands.

Dex rolled and picked himself up. He turned and saw Z charging for him like a freight train. Dex didn't have time to sidestep or defend himself. The creature slammed into him, clasped his hands around Dex's arms, and pushed him farther down the hall. Dex backpedaled to keep from falling over, but he was quickly losing balance. His back foot hit something, and Dex toppled through a giant hole in the floor. He dropped to the floor below, crashing on top of the pile of debris, and rolled off. The air had been knocked out of him.

AUTHOR NOTES: *Conner attempts to lead the Sanders family to safety with help from Quinn, but is that the wisest thing to do, or will it land them in more hot water?*

Chapter 33: Above Ground

A knock sounded at the door, and Conner shuddered. His senses on high alert, he slowly approached. He limped, trying to keep weight off his wounded foot. Reagan and Pam peeked from behind the couch. The compound had been silent from war for a few minutes, and Conner's curiosity was piqued. *Did the good guys win, or did the creatures take over? Can I be sure who is who?*

"Mrs. Sanders?" a muffled voice came from the other side of the door. The tone was that of an older man.

"Who is it?" Conner gripped the AR-15 and prepared to fire.

"It's Quinn. Who is this?"

"This is Conner."

"I'm in here," Reagan called out. "So are my boys and sister."

"We need to abandon the compound," Quinn said. "There's an escape route, but I need you to come quickly."

Conner flung the door open and aimed the rifle at Quinn. The old man was alone in the hall, and his hands rose in surrender at the sight of Conner's gun. Conner glanced left and right down the corridor. It was empty.

"Hurry. We don't have much time," Quinn said.

Conner searched Quinn's eyes. He wasn't sure he could trust him. His instincts warned against it.

"You want to do this?" Conner asked Reagan.

"Yes. We don't have a choice."

She is right. Dammit, he thought. They couldn't stay in this apartment. They had to run to live.

193

They followed Quinn farther into the compound. They turned a couple of times, passed through a meeting room, and came out into another hall. Conner's foot left a trail of blood smears. He hobbled behind the group, protecting their rear in case anyone followed.

"Are you okay?" Pam glanced at Conner's injured foot.

He grimaced and nodded.

Quinn led them to the end of a hallway, where he opened a door. Inside was a small compartment with a ladder that led up through a corrugated tube.

"Up there is our exit." Quinn pointed.

"I'll go first and make sure it's safe," Conner said and turned to Reagan. "You protect the rear?" Reagan knew how to shoot and fight, and he trusted her.

Reagan agreed, and Conner climbed the ladder.

At the top was a lever. Conner turned it, and it unlocked the covering. He pushed it open and quickly popped his head out, pointing the rifle. He saw the abandoned warehouse that sat above the compound a few hundred feet south of him. To the north was a cinder block wall that separated the property lines. It ended fifty feet from the main road. The rest was a barren wasteland of dirt and sagebrush.

"It's clear," he called down. "Send the boys up first then Quinn and Pam. Reagan, you come last."

They were all above ground in a couple of minutes, and Conner turned to Quinn for new directions.

"There are vehicles on the other side of the fence." Quinn pointed at the cinder block wall. "We keep them parked out of sight for occasions like this." He smiled and quickly trotted for the end of the fence line.

"Hold on. Not so fast." Conner limped after him.

"Don't worry. We're safe now," Quinn said triumphantly. He was several feet ahead.

The man moves fast for his age, Conner thought.

"Pull back, Quinn. Wait for us. It might not be safe."

Quinn didn't respond to Conner's warnings. He reached the end of the fence line and crossed beyond into the opening. He turned the corner of the fence and stopped.

Conner quickly planted his feet and motioned for his group to stop. He put a finger to his lips to signal silence. He watched Quinn's reactions. Quinn's smile turned to a frown, and his eyes widened. He slowly began to raise his hands, then gunfire erupted. His body convulsed as several rounds pounded into him. His body crumpled, and Conner saw several bloody holes in his chest and one in his cheek.

THE LANDING SENT SHOCKWAVES of pain throughout Dex's body. Muscles and bones ached, and he struggled to regain his breath. Z stood on the edge of the hole above him, glowering. Z leaped, and Dex rolled off the pile of debris, barely escaping Z's stomping feet.

Dex attempted to stand, but his legs gave way. He quickly crawled away from Z, and with the support of the wall, he was able to rise to his feet again. He twisted to face his opponent, who was rushing him. Z cocked a fist back. Dex knew the impact his punches had. In his condition, he wasn't sure he'd recover.

Instinct took over, and Dex's left arm swung and blocked the blow. His arm felt like a twig about to snap from the impact of the blow, and Z's momentum kept him storming toward him. Adrenalin gave him a newfound strength, and Dex stepped into his opponent with his right foot, body paralleling Z's thrusting fist, and sent a back-elbow blow smashing into Z's face. His triceps squished Z's already-busted nose, and blood droplets flew. Dex then snapped a kick into Z's right kneecap, making it buckle.

Z was already in a motion of retaliation and sent a gut punch that took Dex's strength and air out of him. Z sent two more punches, one to Dex's arm and one to the side of his head. Dex flew and toppled like a rag doll. Lying on his stomach, Dex blew out air that kicked up dust. He pulled his eyes open, but his vision was blurry, and the hall spun before him.

Dragging his broken leg and breathing with heavy rasps, Z approached Dex. His body was severely damaged both internally and externally, but his drive in destroying Dex seemed to fuel him. Z raised his good foot to smash it down on Dex's head. Dex grabbed Z's foot as it came down and pushed. Z's broken leg, which he was using for support, crumpled, and the muscle-bound beast toppled.

Dex rolled away from him and saw a busted pipe sticking out of the wall. He grabbed it and wrenched the pipe free.

He twisted in time to see Z open his mouth, and his inhuman power cry escaped. Dex jabbed one end of the pipe into his throat before the sound could cause disastrous results. Z's eyes widened, and a sickening, choking sound escaped him. Dex pulled the pipe free, and blood flowed, then Dex swung the pipe as hard as he could. Z blocked the pipe with his hand, and his fingers crunched beneath the blow. Z immediately cradled his hurt hand, and Dex swung again, knocking Z's head to the side as the pipe hit his right ear.

Excitement surged through Dex, and he rose to his feet and swung again. Z still sat as his head rocked from the blows, and he was stunned into a stupor. Dex swung and pounded the pipe against his head several times until Z was lying on his side, coughing up blood. His head was a red mess. Z's eyes rolled into the back of his skull, and he stopped breathing.

Dex's shoulders sank, and he dropped the pipe. He stepped away from Z and began to walk back to the hole. His head still spun, and his nerves shook from trauma. He thought of Reagan and the boys and Pam and Conner. He wondered how they were faring. His gut squirmed at the thought of it. He had to make it back to them. But first he had to make it out of this damned place.

He was almost to the hole when something wrapped itself around his neck. It was thin and tight like a whip and scaly like a snake. It pulled him backward and choked him. He twisted to see the horror behind him. Z was standing, but something was off. His head was off, mostly. His left ear sat on his shoulder, hanging on by a stretch of skin, and the Mochvani's midnight-blue head sat in its place. Its silver eyes glowed.

The creature's thin, dark-blue leg popped out below the knee of his broken leg, and a long dark arm shot out from his right wrist, which was now wrapped around Dex's throat. Z's head rolled back and forth on his shoulders, tongue lolling out, threating to fall off at any moment. Z outstretched his other arm, and a tentacle shot out of that one, whipping back and forth wildly.

He snapped his loose tentacle at Dex, and it struck him across the chest like a bullwhip, ripping his skin open. The thing around his neck continued to strangle him, and his eyes bulged. Z whipped him again and again. Dex knew this was his end. His strength was gone, his lungs were about to burst, and he couldn't withstand the pain anymore.

Muffled sounds reached his ears. He heard voices and saw movement. It was a blur of fatigues. It was Cody. He was holding an automatic rifle and firing numerous rounds into the creature that held Dex, and Jon was on the other side, also firing.

Z's body shuddered as it was torn to shreds by bullets. Black pieces of the creature flew as well as the flesh and blood of his human suit. Z's silver eyes dimmed and finally turned to a dark gray. Nothing was left in the Mochvani's life or the body he was half in. Z crumpled into a heap of Mochvani and human flesh. The tentacle around Dex's throat released and dropped. Dex's body wavered like a weed in the wind as his world continued to spin, and he collapsed.

AUTHOR NOTES: *Conner and the family are hiding from a number of men on the other side of the wall, and the odds are against them. Dex and his men attempt to escape the underground bunker to the surface, but it proves tougher than expected and comes with a few surprises.*

Chapter 34: Against the Odds

Conner and his family were crouched behind the block wall. They hadn't been seen. They kept quiet. Conner pressed himself against the wall, trying to listen. He heard the shuffle of feet and the metallic clicking of guns being reloaded. *No voices?* He needed to know how many they were up against.

He gripped his gun at the ready and eyed the opening beyond the end of the wall for any signs of movement. Scenarios played out in Conner's head. If they popped around the corner first, Conner would surprise them and be able to shoot and kill a couple of men. But then the rest would pounce on him, and he didn't see that going well.

If Conner attacked them first, he could easily take out three men, maybe four. He'd have the element of surprise. He'd picked up two hand grenades from the armory. They could give him the edge he needed.

He turned to Pam and Reagan and whispered his plan to them. He expected to see fear in their eyes but was surprised to see hope and bravery. It helped build his.

"I want you all to stay behind this wall until the fighting is over," Conner instructed them.

"I have a gun," Reagan said. "I can help."

"I know. But we can't risk it. If I fail, and they turn the corner and see you, you'll stand a better chance at taking out who's left."

"No." Reagan shook her head. "I'm going in there with you. It's the best defense for us."

"*Trust me.* I'll do better without you." Conner was firm.

199

Reagan nodded reluctantly, and Conner turned to Pam. Her eyes were wet. He leaned in and planted a kiss on her lips. She didn't resist.

"I had to get one in. Just in case." He grinned.

"Just in case *what*?" Pam asked.

He smiled. "In case another man comes along first."

She rolled her eyes, and Conner rose to his feet but kept low.

"Come back to us," Pam said.

"I will." He nodded, armed the grenades, and tossed them over the wall. He aimed his toss in hopes they would land behind the group so he could come at them from the front.

He heard a voice say, "Hey!"

Another one said, "What the hell?"

The grenades blew, and he heard their fragments hit the wall like pellets. Conner was careful to wait until the blasts were complete before attacking. He set his rifle to single shot, pressed the butt against his shoulder, and careened around the corner. He saw a few men amid the dissipating smoke. They stood between two SUVs and the block wall. They shuffled in confusion, and Conner aimed quick and fired fast. He took the first man on his right out with a head shot, shifted to his left, and fired two rounds into another, hitting his chest and throat. Then he charged into the rest of the men and fired two shots into the next guy, and another one on his left lifted his rifle to shoot.

Conner dropped to one knee and shot with precision. One bullet pierced the man's gun hand and exploded out the other side of the rifle he held. Conner's second shot dove into his gut. Conner twisted to shoot at another man who was already firing shots at him. He felt one whiz past his ear, and then something punched his right shoulder.

Conner unloaded five bullets into his enemy then turned back to the man he'd shot in the gut and finished him off with a head shot. The wound in his shoulder screamed for attention, but he ignored it. He took a few steps farther and found two men on the ground. One appeared to have been killed by the grenades, and the other man was crawling. Several wounds from shrapnel peppered his body. Conner shot him in the head along with the dead one, just in case.

He quickly checked all points around him but only saw fallen, dead men. *Seven guys dead.* It was an amazingly good start. Then he heard a car door open. It came from the other side of the SUV and was followed by the padding of boots.

Conner leaped to his feet, ran to the end of the SUV next to him, and hid behind it as bullets fired. Rounds pounded into the SUV's body and busted out windows. Conner's hidden enemy didn't stop. The man bent down and fired shots underneath the vehicle to catch Conner's ankles, but Conner kept on the move. He trotted along the other side of the vehicle, keeping beneath the windows.

The second the shooting paused, Conner set his weapon to automatic fire and let loose hell through the windows of the SUV at the man on the other side. Bullets flew, ricocheted, popped up stuffing from the seats, and broke through more glass, but Conner wasn't sure he'd hit him.

Conner ran to the front of the vehicle, but his wounded foot kept him limping and slow. The pain was intense, and the other man was fast on his tail. Conner hid behind the front grill of the SUV, and his instincts told him it was futile to keep running and hiding. The man would quickly be on him.

Conner had emptied his mag while shooting through the windows. He didn't have time to reload before his attacker was on him. His only hope was to attack first. Despite his foot being on fire and his wounded arm being numb, he charged around the corner of the vehicle and caught the man by surprise.

He used his rifle as a fighting staff and swung the butt of it into the man's left ribs then swung the barrel at his head. It hit the guy's rifle as well as his skull. The man smacked his rifle back at Conner's gun and kicked it out of his hands. Conner grabbed back at his attacker's rifle and wrestled it from his hands, and soon they were fighting fist to fist. Conner jabbed a knee into the man's gut, and the man's fist nicked Conner's chin. Conner came back with a left knuckle punch to the guy's throat.

Conner quickly unsheathed the knife secured by his belt and, using his left hand, stabbed it at the man's neck, but his enemy blocked it and kicked Conner away from him with his right foot. While Conner stumbled, his opponent reached for a pistol in his pants, and Conner dove at him and raked his gun hand with the knife and then swung the blade and jabbed it into the side of his neck. He quickly withdrew it and stabbed it in and out of his neck several times to ensure a quicker death.

The man fell limp in his arms and crumpled. Conner stood over him, panting. He turned and hobbled away from him. Blood from the gunshot covered his entire arm, and his foot screamed at him to quit fucking walking.

He stepped around the SUV and saw a tall black figure holding a rifle. It was a Mochvani. The creature had slithered out of its dead host and picked up a gun. It had only seconds of life left in it, but it was going to fight until the bitter end. Two other black creatures lay on the ground like sludges of oil, but a second one was rising to its feet, too, and picked up a gun.

"Shit." Conner sighed.

A gunshot rang out, and Conner thought it was meant for him, but then he saw the creature shudder. Reagan had turned the corner of the wall and begun firing at the Mochvani. She fired several more shots into it then quickly shot at the second one. The bullets didn't seem to have a killing effect on them, but they did stun them and kept them from attacking. The rounds pierced their bodies as if they consisted of thick Jell-O. Pieces of their black flesh flew out the backs of their bodies. They soon began to choke. Their silver eyes flickered, and the bodies sank to the ground.

Reagan turned to Conner. "Are you okay?"

He nodded and gestured for her to hand him the gun. She tossed it to him, and Conner walked back to the one he'd stabbed and shot at the black creature that crawled out of him until it didn't move anymore.

AUTHOR NOTES: *Dex finished his fight against Z, and it's taken nearly everything out of him. His men come to his rescue, and together, they work to escape the building before it collapses.*

Chapter 35: Bus Assault

"Can you make it?" Cody asked Dex.

Dex was sitting on the ground, gathering his wits. The world still spun but not as fast. He took a deep breath and nodded. "You found guns?"

"Yes," Cody said. "We ran into a group that was wounded by the blast. They were trying to get away. We killed them and stole their guns."

"Badger? Hawkins?" Dex asked.

"Badger will live. But Hawkins..." He shook his head with grave eyes. "Let's get you upstairs."

Dex looked at the giant hole in the ceiling and wondered how he'd climb out of it. He felt like he'd been run over by a truck.

Cody and Jon helped him to his feet, and within a few minutes, they were together again on the upper floor. Much of Dex's strength was returning to him, and they quickly marched their way to the exit. Badger leaned on Jon and Dex. Badger was in bad shape. Dex knew they had to get medical help for him soon. Cody and Roberto led the way, and Shields and Bing protected their rear.

Dex pulled his shirt over his nose and mouth. Others did the same or pressed their mouths against their arms. The smoke was thick, and the fire was spreading. His eyes burned. Pieces of the floor were gone, and they had to watch their step. The walls and flooring creaked. The damage had decimated a lot of the compound, and Dex wondered if it would collapse on them before they managed to escape.

Level after level, they met no resistance. There were cracks and broken windows from the explosion, but the farther they got from ground zero, the less damage there was. Dex didn't have a good feeling. *It can't be this easy.*

He withdrew his iPhone and texted Reagan. *We're alive. How are you? Are you safe?* He didn't have any signal, so the message didn't send, but he knew once he reached the outside, it would.

They walked the final hall to the end. They entered the doorway, climbed the stairwell, and exited through the door and into the motel bathroom. It was empty and silent. Cody and Dex shared wary looks.

Cody motioned for Roberto to follow him. They darted into the bedroom, aiming their guns, and froze. What Dex feared the most was written on Cody's face. Dex and Jon set Badger on the toilet seat.

"Sit here for a moment, bud," Dex said to Badger, who nodded while gritting his teeth in pain. His face was shades of white and gray. His wounds needed attention fast.

Dex turned the corner into the bedroom and saw what Cody and Jon were staring at through the front window. A fleet of men stood in rows along the parking lot. Dex walked closer to the window and saw a tall man standing at the center, physician's coat flapping in the breeze. Dr. H stood at the helm, and he wore a pretentious grin.

"None of them are armed!" Jon exclaimed.

"What are we waiting for?" Roberto approached the window with his rifle raised. Dex knew why they weren't armed, and he was a second too late to warn Roberto.

There were at least fifty men in the parking lot, and in unison, their eyes turned and focused on Roberto, and their mouths dropped open. Their shrieks shook the air and pierced Dex's ears, and Roberto's gun exploded. Fragments of it flew into his hands and face, and he fell back.

"Stalemate," Cody grumbled.

"No." Dex shook his head. "We're sitting ducks in here."

Badger crawled into the bedroom and leaned on the wall to reach a standing position. "What the *hell*?"

"You okay?" Jon asked Roberto.

Roberto rose to his feet, cradling his wounded arms, and nodded. Jagged pieces of metal stuck out from bloody wounds in his cheeks and forehead.

Ideas churned in Dex's head. He flipped through several different scenarios, none of which looked good. He crossed to the back of the motel room. There was a small, rectangular window. It looked barely big enough to fit a body through.

"You have something?" Cody asked.

"Maybe," Dex mumbled.

His phone vibrated. It was Reagan.

SOOO glad you're alive! We're okay now. Where are you? It was followed by heart emojis.

Relief flooded and warmed his body. Reagan and the boys were alive. He'd imagined the worst. He hesitated in responding, not knowing what to say, then finally wrote, *We're in the motel room. About to clear it. I'll call you soon when we're on the road. I love you. Give my love to the boys.*

She wrote back with hearts and a kissy-face emoji.

Dex turned to his men. "Does anyone know how to hotwire a school bus?"

"I've hotwired most things. Not a bus before, but I'm sure I can figure it out," Shields said.

"Shields, you come with me. The rest of you stay here and keep them busy. I want all their attention on you guys. If they see what Shields and I are doing, we don't stand a chance," Dex said.

Shields followed Dex to the back window. He'd just begun smashing the glass out when the shrill screams began again and pierced his ears. The floor rumbled. Dex felt the vibration below his feet, and then he saw the walls shaking back and forth. Pictures fell off the walls and the dressers, and the bed bounced.

Roberto ran to the front window and tossed a grenade into the air. The room stopped shaking as the Mochvani refocused their energy on the grenade. It exploded in midair before it had the chance to reach them.

Shields crawled through the back window and called back to Dex, "Clear."

Dex looked back at Roberto, whose body was rising in the air by the Mochvani's unseen force. He floated two feet above the floor, and then came crunching sounds. Roberto screamed in pain and clutched his chest. *Are they breaking his bones?*

"Go!" Cody yelled at Dex.

Dex wasted no more time. He leaped through the window and dropped to the ground outside, where Shields waited. They quickstepped north to the end of the building. The motel was shaped like an L, and when they got to the end of it, it turned south. Fortunately, there was an open corridor between the buildings that led to the front parking lot. Ice and vending machines stood in the corridor.

They progressed to the end of the hallway, stopped, and crouched before entering the open. The school bus was still there. It stood between them and the Mochvani. They were fortunate for that.

"Shit. The door's on the other side," Shields hissed.

"We can do it. Keep low as you turn the corner, and get inside as quickly as you can. I'll be right behind you," Dex said.

Shields agreed.

They both trotted to the front grill of the vehicle, and Dex peeked around the corner. He saw the group of Mochvani standing in their human suits, all of them facing the motel room. The ground trembled from the force that shook room eight. He heard the snapping of wood and glass shattering as the Mochvani continued their screeching assault.

There were a group of men only twenty feet from Dex and Shields. Any misstep or sound would alert them. Shields quickly stepped around the corner, into the open, and pushed to open the bus door. It squeaked, and Shields' back foot slipped as he entered, and his shin slammed against the step. He grunted in pain.

The sounds were low but loud enough for one man to turn. He locked eyes on Dex. Dex lifted his rifle and fired several shots. The bullets dove into the man's chest, and then Dex aimed at the next man and fired several shots into him. The first two men crumpled with bloody holes. Dex shifted and fired several shots at a third man before diving into the bus.

The ground stopped shaking, and so did the crunching sounds of the motel attack. The enemies shifted their focus onto the school bus.

Shields was in the driver's seat, searching for the wires to start the engine, when his face lit up. "The keys are in the ignition!" He turned the key, and the engine cranked but didn't start.

Of course.

The high-pitched sound started again, and the large vehicle began to rock back and forth. Shields turned the key again, and the engine roared to life. Windows in the bus burst and showered Dex with shards of glass. Shields shifted the bus into reverse, but they didn't move. He pushed on the gas pedal, revving the engine, but it didn't budge. The tires squealed, and the smell of burnt rubber filled the air.

Amid the screeches of the Mochvani, Dex heard rapid gunfire. He popped his head up and saw his men firing from the front window of room eight. Their front door flew open, and Cody stepped out, spreading lead. With the focus of the creatures on Dex and Shields, it freed up his men to fire on the Mochvani.

The bus stopped shaking, and Dex turned to Shields. "Punch it!"

Released from the invisible force, the school bus shot into reverse like a rocket and plowed through the enemy. Several bodies flew and crumpled beneath the monolithic vehicle. Shields yanked hard on the steering wheel, turning the bus until the front grill faced west instead of east. Dex heard the thumps of bodies slamming against the side of the bus as it raked through them all.

Shields lurched the bus forward, stopped in front of room eight, and pushed on the lever to open the door. The rest of their team burst from the room and jumped into the bus. Cody helped Badger, who tried his best to hurry despite his wounds.

Jon and Bing raced to the back of the bus and began firing out the windows. Shields slammed the door closed once Cody and Badger were in. Badger collapsed into a seat, and Cody plopped into another one. Dex stepped next to Shields, who shifted into drive.

A man rose to his feet on the asphalt before them. It was Dr. H. Blood ran from his eyes, nose, and mouth, and his clothes were rumpled and body scraped. Black tips of tentacles poked out from his nostrils and mouth.

"Goodbye, Dr. H.," Dex said.

Shields floored the gas. Dex heard the thumps beneath them as they rolled over the son of a bitch.

AUTHOR NOTES: *The Bus Assault chapter was so much fun to write because I didn't know how this story would finish until I was writing it. These ideas popped out as I wrote them onto the page, and I felt that it was a perfect battle scene for our heroes to go through. Conner and Reagan finished killing off the men between them and their escape vehicle, but where will they go now?*

Chapter 36: Second Life

Conner brushed pebbles of broken glass off the seats of the SUV, and Reagan, Pam, and the boys piled in. He took one more look around before sliding behind the driver's seat. A strong breeze blew clouds of dust around them, but no one was in sight. The bodies they'd taken out stayed dead where they'd dropped. He started the engine and drove out onto the main road and headed for the warehouse.

"Where are you going?" Reagan asked.

"Back to the compound. We have to see if anyone else made it."

"That could be dangerous. What if those creatures are there?"

"Then I'll keep driving. But we have to check. We need them," Conner said.

They approached the entrance to the compound and saw dead bodies strewn about. Black smoke clouded most of the grisly scene. It was pouring from fires burning just inside the front doors. Conner saw movement and stopped the vehicle. He gripped his pistol and tensed.

"Conner!" Pam cried.

Figures walked out from the smoke, holding rifles pointed at them.

I'll slam on the gas and plow through these assholes if I have to, Conner thought. *But how will you know? You won't be able to tell if they're human or Silver Eyes. Reagan was right. This was a bad idea.*

The man in the lead was huge. He wore fatigues and a handlebar mustache. Blood smeared half his face. He stopped short of the SUV, pointing his rifle at Conner.

"It's the guy who helped us in the mess hall and took us to the armory," Conner said.

"Let's hope it's still *him*," Pam said.

"Step out!" the soldier demanded.

Conner weighed his options. Even if he knew they were Silver Eyes, and he hit the gas and drove through them, the large soldier pointing the rifle would fill him with lead before he had the chance. Conner had to concede. He exited the vehicle with his hands up.

"It's us," Conner said. "We're friends. You helped us inside the compound."

The big man lowered the gun slightly and eyed him.

"You're the guy who took out the terrorist. You saved lives."

Conner grinned. "That's me."

"But how do I know for sure?" the soldier asked.

"When a Silver Eye takes over a human, they don't retain the human's memories. I remember you, and you remember me. That's a good sign."

"You're right." The man lowered his weapon. "Then you won't mind if I check your eyes, and then you can check mine. Just to be sure."

Relief overwhelmed Conner, and he sighed in relief. "Sounds good to me."

DR. H OPENED HIS EYES. Pain ricocheted throughout his body. He lay stomach down on the asphalt and turned his head to one side. He wasn't sure he could move any of his limbs. They felt disjointed and mangled. He was nothing but a torn-up rag doll. He saw his left arm was bent the wrong way, as if someone had snapped it like a twig. His waist was twisted around, and he couldn't feel his legs. This was the end for him. He couldn't heal from this.

He heard the shuffling of feet, and he craned his eyes to see a man approaching. It was one of his. He appeared healthy and unscathed. Dr. H tried to move his arm, but it did nothing. He urged his hand to move, and finally, his fingers curled. He tried to speak and coughed up blood.

The man stopped and looked down at him.

"H-Help...me!" Dr. H cried.

The man crouched next to his head.

"Dr. H?" the man asked. He ran his eyes up and down his body. "You are hurt bad."

"Come... closer," Dr. H said, and the man leaned in. "Relinquish your vessel."

The man hesitated.

"For the cause," Dr. H said.

The man remained motionless.

"That's an order."

The man pressed his eyes closed and clenched his teeth. After a couple of minutes, a black finger popped out of his ear. It stretched, and more of the black sludge of the Mochvani exited like beef from a meat grinder. Dr. H departed his own host through its mouth, and his dark Mochvani stretched to the man's opposite ear and entered. Two more fingers stretched out from Dr. H and dove into the man's nostrils and mouth. The man's body shuddered as Dr. H consumed it entirely. His Mochvani surrounded the bones and organs of its new vessel and melded itself to the skeleton.

Dr. H stood in his new body. It was a bit shorter than he was used to, but it had more strength. *Not bad,* he thought. He looked down at the writhing, dying Mochvani. His silver eyes looked at Dr. H in pain. Dr. H turned without a care and walked away. He had a mission to finish.

There were other survivors. He discovered four of his men completely whole and five who were wounded but still able to walk. He grouped them together.

Follow me, he said telepathically and synced their thoughts. He led his men to the north end of the motel, the opposite wing from where room eight sat, and opened the door to room one. The interior had been turned into a garage. They had knocked down several of the walls to extend the space. Five vehicles were parked inside. Dr. H and the men climbed into two of the black SUVs. The wall before them slid open, and the vehicles drove out.

Dr. H turned onto the highway and sped west. The night was upon them. The storm had moved in, and the clouds couldn't hold the rain any longer and burst their bellies open. Droplets pounded the windshield.

Dr. H had men stationed at The Flying J truck stop a mile out. They acted as sentries and kept their eyes out for any oncoming danger. He called to them.

Have you seen them? he asked.

They had. He knew where they were. Adrenalin surged through him like electricity. The rage inside escalated to a point of explosion. He would rain vengeance on them all. Those stinking, pathetic humans. For so long, he'd had to hide inside their disgusting bodies. One would think after so many years, he'd be used to it, but he wasn't. Their bodies were restrictive and vile. Humans had a smell that made him gag, and he had to live in it every day. He had to pander to these *things* and pretend to be one of them. It made him sick.

The sanctuary they'd built had been a home for them—a haven where they could be who they really were, without fear or threat. The humans had destroyed that and had killed many of his friends. He was unbound now. Nothing was going to hold him back.

The tail end spun as he slammed on the brakes to turn into the truck stop. Water sprayed from the road, but he steadied the vehicle and pulled to a stop next to the gas pumps. The second SUV parked behind him.

On the east side of the parking lot were three Hummers, and next to them was the yellow school bus from the motel. It was parked askew. *They are here.* The rest of the parking places were all filled except for one or two, and behind the truck stop sat several semis. The establishment was busy with many humans.

A blue Toyota sat parked alone on the west end of the lot, and two men exited and trotted to Dr. H as he stepped out of the SUV. The two men stopped short of Dr. H and gave him a questioning look.

"It's me. I'm in a different vessel," H told them.

"I saw them enter the front doors not twenty minutes ago," one of the men said while pointing at the entrance.

Dr. H turned and took two steps toward the store and then stopped. Lights were on inside, and rain poured down the windows. The building was larger than most gas stations. It was a retreat for truck drivers and had a small shopping store, showers in the bathrooms, and a full diner attached. He was going to tear the building into pieces and obliterate everyone inside.

His men stood in a straight line on either side of him. He centered his focus. Each man's mouth dropped open in unison, and their shrieks split the silence, and the force of their voices pounded against the truck stop. The front windows and doors exploded in a high-pitched shattering of glass, and the building shook.

Dr. H dropped his jaw beyond the normal human capacity. It disjointed itself like a boa constrictor preparing to swallow its prey. From his maw protruded the dark head of his Mochvani. Its silver eyes glowed. His foreign head split in four ways and opened like a flower. Four triangular pieces, like petals, spread out to reveal a pinkish interior filled with rows of sharp teeth. His head now mimicked a Venus flytrap but was much darker and more menacing. From this new head escaped a shriek that rose over the rest and amplified the sound tenfold.

Bricks of the building blew apart. Cash registers split, and aisles of food blasted apart, throwing clouds of chips, candy bars, snacks, cans of food, and a million other items into the air. The refrigerators and frozen sections burst in an array of glass and fluids. Chairs and tables in the diner busted and flew, and then the gas range exploded into a ball of fire and smoke, blowing a gaping hole in the roof.

Embers rained down, and the building began to sink in on itself like a caved-in cake. Dr. H sent the entire force of his rage like a battering ram into the structure, and the rest of the walls burst into flying, burning pieces in all directions.

Exhausted and spent, each man closed his mouth. The shrieks fell silent, and all that rent the night were the sounds of a million particles falling to earth and the crackle of flames. What wasn't blown in pieces and lying in piles of embers and debris stood like a blackened skeleton of what the truck stop used to be.

They have to be dead, Dr. H thought. *But where are the bodies?*

AUTHOR NOTES: *Second Life was added after I'd finished drafting the whole story. After the bus rolled over Dr. H, that was supposed to be it. However, I felt that it was too easy. Dr. H wasn't going to go down that easy, so Second Life was the best title for this chapter. I'm really happy with how this turned out. Sometimes more is better, but did our heroes really die? You'll have to read the next chapter to find out. I'm not opposed to writing sad endings or killing main characters off.*

Chapter 37: Surprise

Twenty-five minutes prior, Shields drove into the parking lot of the Flying J truck stop and parked the bus behind the Hummers. There was no real spot for it, and he didn't care. They filed out of the bus with sore limbs and battered bodies.

"I could use something to drink," Shields said.

"I gotta take a piss. If someone can help me," Badger said.

"Sorry, bud. You gotta hold your dick yourself." Jon grimaced.

"Guys. We need to take precautions. This isn't over," Dex said.

"What do you mean?" Cody asked.

"We didn't kill all of them back there. They could show up any minute."

"He's right. I saw a few stragglers when we tore out of there," Jon said.

"What should we do?" Cody asked.

"Do you still have those grenade launchers?"

"Yes," Cody said.

Dex turned to the truck stop. Several people were coming and going. The gas pumps were full of people filling their tanks. The place was crowded.

"We have to get these people out of here."

"They're not going to all fit in the bus," Jon said.

"I have another idea. Jon, you round up everybody who's outside. Including everyone at the pumps. Tell them to move their cars. Shields and Bing, you guys clear the diner, and Cody and I will clear the rest of the place."

"What about me?" Badger asked.

"You stay over here in this field." Jon pointed at the empty space behind their parked vehicles. The ground sloped into an empty lot. "We'll bring everyone over to this field and hide behind this berm. You'll be here to welcome them. You can take a piss while you wait."

They agreed to the plan and moved fast. The men entered the store like a hurricane, carrying weapons.

Dex fired a few rounds into the ceiling, and people throughout the store turned in horror.

"I need everyone's attention! This is an emergency! We're not here to harm you, but people who will are coming! I need everyone to head out the back door. Now!"

Most of the people stood with wide eyes like deer in headlights. Others ducked under tables and ran into the bathrooms. Dex couldn't blame them. They didn't know who he was or that he was there to save them. For all they knew, he was a terrorist. But he also didn't have time to explain. He fired a couple more shots.

"Move it now!" Cody hollered.

Shields and Bing were rounding people up in the diner. Dex heard them yelling similar demands. Jon was outside, herding his crowd. A couple of people ran for the front door, and Dex stopped them.

"No! Out the back door, folks!"

They rounded up the people quicker and more efficiently than Dex had imagined. A couple of guys were carrying guns and tried to make a move, but Cody caught them in time and forced them to surrender. The people funneled out the back door, and they got bottlenecked a couple of times. They ushered people to the east-side field behind the berm and told them all to get down and keep their mouths shut.

DR. H CLOSED HIS MOCHVANI head and sucked it back inside his mouth. He stared at the burning rubble before him. He didn't see any bodies—not an arm, a leg, or a foot. He turned to his informant with a baleful glare.

"Where are they?" he snarled.

The man shrugged and stuttered, "I-I saw them go in. No one came out. I swear. One of them was…" The man's eyes widened.

"Was what?"

"He was outside, telling everybody to move. People moved their cars and then followed him over there." He pointed to the east, and Dr. H turned in the direction he was pointing. "But he was the only one. The rest of them never came out."

A figure stepped out from behind a line of vehicles. He was alone and aiming a rifle.

"Dex," Dr. H hissed.

All of Dr. H's men turned to face Dex.

"What do you plan to do with *that*?" Dr. H mocked him.

Dex grinned and pointed at him. "Dr. H? Is that you? You look different."

"I'm surprised you can tell it is me."

"I always recognize an asshole."

Dr. H sneered, opened his mouth, and shot a sound vibration strong enough to flip the weapon from Dex's hands and throw him off his feet. Then Dr. H heard a couple of reports from behind him—not quite like a gun but something different. They came from the west side of the parking lot. He turned in time to see two men holding grenade launchers aimed at them, and the projectiles they had fired were heading straight for them. No, not for *them*—for the gas pumps next to them. Dex had been a diversion. He had kept all attention away from the real threat.

Dr. H and his men opened their mouths to send sound vibrations and destroy the grenades, but they were too late.

The explosions thundered and lit up the sky with balls of fire and smoke. Dr. H and his men were instantly engulfed and propelled several feet. Fiery plumes of mushroom clouds curled high in the air. More blasts erupted as each pump was triggered by the fire, like dominos.

THE HEAT WAVE THAT hit Dex was immense, and he felt it singe his arm hairs and eyebrows. The sounds of the explosions rang in his ears for several minutes, and he was temporarily blinded by the flashes of light. He turned his gaze away and covered his ears until the blasts finally receded.

He stood and turned to the wreckage. Plumes of black smoke filled the air, and the fires burned furiously. He looked for Dr. H's body and his men. He saw smoking black lumps surrounding the blast area. As he stepped closer, he could see the outlines of their scorched skeletons. He felt confident that they were finished.

He turned to face the crowd of people hunkered behind the berm. The light of the flames flickered across their faces. Most were men, but some were women, a few were children, and a handful were teens. Each of them wore a shocked expression. Some were in tears, some shaking in fear, and others sat in awe. *They saw.*

"What the hell was that?" a tall man in a flannel shirt and a ball cap asked.

"Are we going to die next?" a young girl cried.

"We need some answers," another man demanded.

More people started to murmur and comment, and Dex motioned for them to be quiet.

"We are not your enemy," he assured them. "What you saw there"—he pointed at the wreckage—"they were the enemy. Unfortunately, there're many more of them. This is just the beginning. If we're going to survive this, you all need to know the truth, and you need to spread it. Do not forget what you saw here today."

Dex let out a breath and looked across the crowd. He felt a glimmer of hope, knowing they had more people on their side—people who had witnessed the truth and, with any luck, would help.

AUTHOR NOTES: *Okay, so I kept our heroes alive, and they surprised our villains. I couldn't do that to Reagan and the kids. Dex had to survive. For now. Dex and his men are driving to the designated safe house.*

Chapter 38: Safe House

It had been agreed upon by all parties to meet at a safe house near Castle Rock, Colorado, if anything went wrong, and shit had gone wrong. Dex talked with Reagan on the phone while Shields drove. Each filled the other in. Dex and his men pulled up to the farmhouse near midnight. He saw silhouettes of people on the front porch, and it didn't take him long to discern they were his family.

Reagan and the boys ran into Dex's arms. He hugged and kissed them as if he'd they'd spent years apart, not hours.

"Come on, Dad. Let's show you the house. It's huge." Jacob grabbed Dex's hand and began to lead him.

"Yeah, we have our own bedroom with a TV and everything!" Noah exclaimed.

Their excitement was infectious. Dex smiled and snatched Reagan's hand, and they both followed the boys with fond smiles. Conner sat in a chair on the porch, Pam next to him. His leg was wrapped, and his arm hung in a sling. Dex approached him.

"Go on to your room. We'll be up shortly," Dex told his boys, and they ran off. He turned to Conner. "Reagan told me what you did."

"She told you I got shot?" Conner raised his eyebrows.

"You saved my wife and kids. Again."

"And me," Pam threw in. "Don't forget about me."

"No one could forget about you, hon." Conner shot her a wink.

Dex noticed Conner holding Pam's hand. Dex thought about all Conner had done for him. The loyalty and sacrifice he had shown went far beyond friendship. How could he ever repay him?

"No one could ask for a better brother. I'm glad you're part of this family." Dex shook his hand then leaned in and gave him a kiss on the forehead.

"Did you just kiss me? Good thing I didn't save the world. What would you give me then?"

"Just more hugs," Dex said, and they both chuckled, then Dex got serious and teared up. "But really, thank you. My family is my world."

"Mine too, brotha." Conner nodded.

Jon and Bing helped carry Badger into the dining room. It had been turned it into a makeshift infirmary. Dex and Reagan followed them in. Dex checked on Badger and expressed his gratitude to his men, as did Reagan. Reagan and Dex left the kitchen and stepped into the hall.

"Another group met us here. They're from California. Fortunately, they have a doctor and a nurse among them. We lost so many people back at the compound," Reagan pointed out.

"I'm so sorry, Reagan. That must have been hell. I shouldn't have left you."

"You were where you needed to be. We both agreed to that. We had Conner. And Quinn. He led us out of there."

"I can't believe he's gone," Dex said sadly.

"What do we do now?" Reagan asked as they found a couch in the family room and sat down.

Dex sighed heavily, wishing he had the answers. "I don't know. We can't go back to our house. It's not safe."

"We can't go back to our *lives*," Reagan said.

Dex leaned forward and stared at the ground. They had won the battle they set out to win. The Mochvani's underground bunker, the canyon village they used as a refuge, and the portal were all obliterated. But he knew that wasn't all of them. There were more. The creatures had infected the world, and there wasn't any way of knowing their true numbers. And he had to believe there were more doorways to their world in other places.

Two cowboy boots planted themselves in Dex's line of vision, and inside the boots stood a tall man. Dex craned his neck to look up at him. The man appeared to be in his midfifties and had a full head of hair that was dark brown and part gray with a matching beard. He stuck a hand out, and Dex shook it.

The man's eyes gleamed, and a wide smile spread across his face. "Dex."

"Yes. Do I know you?" The man looked familiar, but Dex couldn't place him.

"David Tolham. This is my group. We came from California. Quinn called me a couple of days ago and said he needed my help. Sorry we're late."

"Nice to meet you, David. Your help is much appreciated. I'm glad you have a medical team."

"You don't remember me, do you?"

Dex squinted. A slight smile pulled the side of David's face, and it was unmistakable. *Could it be?* he thought. *Could this really be Jack Bennett?*

"David Tolham is the name I go by now. I went by a different name years ago."

"Jack?" Dex asked.

The man nodded.

The word dropped like a lead ball in Dex's stomach. It took a few seconds for it to sink in. All the recognition came flooding back.

Jack spread his arms for a hug. He didn't get one. Instead, Dex stood up and walked past him. Reagan jumped up and followed.

Dex stopped at the archway that led into the hall and turned to face Jack. "I liked you better when you were David Tolham."

AUTHOR NOTES: *I wasn't originally going to bring Jack Bennett back into the story, but he had become a vital component in Dex's life, and it*

made sense. After all that Dex had been through, and with his mind still processing a previous life he didn't know about, of course he'd be pissed to find out Jack was still alive. He had trusted in this man as a father figure, and he needed him in his life, and Jack had abandoned him.

Chapter 39: The Ending Is Just the Beginning

Dex walked into the kitchen and opened the fridge, feeling the cold air on his face, his eyes wandering across the shelves.

"No beer? I could really use a beer right about now," Dex said.

"There's water." Reagan stepped next to him and pointed at a pack of water bottles on the bottom shelf.

"Is there alcohol in them?"

Reagan chuckled at the absurdity.

Dex shrugged and grabbed one. "Do you want one?"

"No, I'm good," she said.

"Dex." Bennett approached. "I'm sorry. Did I say something that offended you?"

Dex turned with an expression that said, *Really? Are you serious?*

"I don't want to talk right now."

Dex brushed past him, and Bennett followed.

"Dex, if it's about how I left..."

"*How you left?* You didn't just leave, Jack. You never came back. And then they told me you were dead."

Bennett sighed and nodded.

"I lost my best friend, then I lost my parents, and then I *lost* you. *You* were all I had left in the world. You didn't think that would affect me? My life has been turned upside down and inside out. To learn that you've been alive this whole time but kept me out of your life is really shitty. Why didn't you come back?"

Behind his thoughts, Dex knew he was losing it. Emotions that had been trapped for years were resurfacing—more like exploding.

"I'm really sorry, Dex. It's not what any of us intended. I did what I thought was best at the time. I had to pretend I was dead to protect you and everyone I loved. It killed me to leave you behind. Our group was compromised. They were after me, and they were after you. We lost a lot of good men and women, and everything we'd built was scattered. It took years to rebuild it all." Bennett's eyes were somber.

Dex remained silent while staring at the floor.

"I have a wife and kids, Jack. We were living a normal life until those freaks took us and tortured us. Nothing is the same anymore. We've lost our home, our jobs, our *lives*. And from now on, we have to live like renegades, looking over our shoulders every minute of the day. If that's not enough, you come waltzing in, and guess what? You're not dead anymore."

"Your life has been one big shit show. I get it. And I'm sorry. I made mistakes, and I should never have left you. I know that. Hindsight is twenty-twenty. But we have a chance to start again, and I need you. We all do."

Dex thought for a moment. He didn't want to continue this conversation anymore. He was still upset with Jack, but deep inside, he wanted to wrap his arms around him, and that made him angrier. He wanted to stay mad at him. "So what's next?" Dex asked.

"Well, we're still regrouping. I have two more groups expected to arrive in the next couple of days. Then we begin to plan our next move." Bennett withdrew his phone and opened an image. It was a picture of a sharp-looking man with white-and-gray hair. "Do you recognize this man?"

"That's the guy running for the state senate, right? I've seen his ads," Dex said.

"Henry Patterson. He's expected to win. Our sources say he's working for the Mochvani."

"That means they're infecting our government. That could change everything."

"Yes, and the group of Silver Eyes he works for is a much larger group than the one you just dealt with. The threat is becoming more dangerous. They'll be able to make changes and decisions in their favor. They'll be harder to find and even harder to touch."

"So we become assassins," Dex grumbled. He unscrewed the cap from his water bottle and took a drink.

"Essentially, yes," Bennett said. "There's someone I want you to meet. He's going to be a big help to us."

Bennett turned his head as a man in his early thirties entered. He was slightly shorter than Dex, with a receding hairline, and he wore a tight T-shirt that reflected a muscular body beneath it. He smiled as he approached him with an outstretched hand. His eyes were soft with humility, and Dex got the sense that he was a simple, grounded man. He had a feeling that he could trust him.

"Dex, I want you to meet Link Balsey."

Dex shook his hand. His grip was tight.

"Nice to meet you," Link said.

"You too," Dex replied.

"Link has dealt with a similar form of Mochvani. However, these creatures were from a different world from the Silver Eyes, and they come with a far more dangerous power. Link's been able to find their weakness and defeat many of them."

Link shrugged with embarrassment. "You make it sound like I'm a superhero. I just got lucky."

"Whatever you call it, you're going to be a big help to us," Bennett said. "You might recall his story. It was splashed across the country's media a few years back."

"I hired these demons to help a woman kill her brother. I thought he was her abusive husband and that she loved me." His eyes shifted to the ground. "Hardly a hero."

"I do remember that story. I recall you hiring a hitman, but there was no mention of demons or otherworldly things."

"No, there wouldn't be, would there?"

"Right," Dex said, nodding knowingly.

"I'm glad I found your group. I was tracking down demons in California when I came across David Tolham. The demons turned out to be Mochvani."

"Dex." Jack hooked a thumb toward Link. "Link's got a talent—a gift, really—in tracking the Mochvani."

Dex's head spun. He didn't know what to think. It was a lot of information to take in at once. He took in a deep breath and let it out. "If you'll excuse me, Link, this is a lot to process. I'm going to tuck in my boys."

"Of course. You and your family get some rest. We'll talk in the morning." Bennett smiled and walked away with Link.

Dex turned to Reagan and rolled his eyes. She wrapped her arms around him, and they held each other in a tight embrace.

"We'll be okay," she whispered to him. "Do you need a Xanax?"

"Yes."

DEX TURNED THE TV OFF as Reagan pulled the covers up to their boys' chins. Both Noah and Jacob were in and out of sleep. She gave them each a kiss, and so did Dex.

On their way out, Jacob asked, "Dad? Did you get all the bad guys?"

Dex stopped and turned. He wanted to provide his kids with as much security as possible. They were too young to deal with the stress and anxiety of the situation. They'd been through enough already, and there was probably more to come.

He didn't know where they'd go from here. All Dex was sure of was that life would never be the same. They'd always be on the run and looking over their shoulders. They couldn't trust anyone completely. He also knew that Jack Bennett oversaw this group now, and as much as he hated it, as angry as he was with him, he knew that Bennett was the best protection his family had right now.

He glanced at Reagan, who had a look of the same resolution in her eyes. He turned to the boys again.

"Yes. We got them all. Sleep tight." He turned the light off and left the door open a crack to let some light in. "Love you, boys."

AUTHOR NOTES: *I'm sure you can tell that I'm not done. I have way too much story left to tell. The Intruders fits into The Other Side Cycle. It's a stand-alone but is also connected to elements in my other books, both written and not yet written. It all began with The Other Side of Elsewhere. The parallel world introduced in that story leads to a highway of alternate universes. There are spots throughout our world where the veil between our universe and other worlds is thin, and occasionally, unknown species come through. They will spawn their own stories, where brave men and women will have to stand and fight. You may recognize characters from my other books who will intersect with others, such as Link. If you've read The Other Side of Elsewhere, and you're wondering if we'll see Ret McCoy again, the answer is yes. I'm not through with him. Thank you again for reading The Intruders, and I look forward to hearing from you in reviews and correspondence through my monthly newsletters.*

About the Author

When Brett McKay isn't conjuring demons and bloodthirsty psychopaths to put on paper, he sells landscaping. He loves all types of music, but hard rock and heavy metal fuel him the most. He enjoys the outdoors, spending time with friends and family, and curling up in front of a good movie with his wife and a bucket of popcorn.

Brett lives in Utah with his wife and two sons. Fall is his favorite time of year because he gets to decorate his house for Halloween much too early for his neighbors.

Read more at https://www.brettmckaybooks.com/.

About the Publisher

Dear Reader,

We hope you enjoyed this book. Please consider leaving a review on your favorite book site.

Visit https://RedAdeptPublishing.com to see our entire catalogue.

Check out our app for short stories, articles, and interviews. You'll also be notified of future releases and special sales.